Love Lifted Me

Lisa Washington

Library of Congress Control Number: 2019905375

ISBN-13: 978-0-9998871-4-1
ISBN-10: 0-9998871-4-9

All Scripture quotations, unless otherwise indicated, are taken from the Holy Bible, New International Version®, NIV®. Copyright ©1973, 1978, 1984, 2011 by Biblica, Inc.™ Used by permission of Zondervan. All rights reserved worldwide. www.zondervan.com The "NIV" and "New International Version" are trademarks registered in the United States Patent and Trademark Office by Biblica, Inc.™

Book Cover Design by Angie

Washington Way Publishing
P.O. Box 7231
Fishers, IN 46038
Printed in the United States of America
www.thewashingtonwayllc.com

DEDICATION

To my Girls

Table of Contents

Lisa Washington

ACKNOWLEDGMENTS

My Love, My Husband

Dr. Rickey & Robyn McCray

My Mama Brenda Sims

Lena Pryor

Scott & April Sims

Rasheda Randle

Book Cover Designer Angie

Graphic Designer Taco GFX

Chapter 1

"Angel, keep your eyes open. The informant said we'd know him when we see him."

"Copy that, Civic."

Darkness filled the room and smoke seeped from the vents. Someone was trying to make visibility near impossible. Nehemiah switched to his night vision goggles. He was perched just inside of the furnace room in the back of the hotel's ballroom. He counted 22 hostages and 4 shooters. The smoke was making it difficult for Nehemiah to keep his eyes on the target.

"Angel, come in."

"Go, Civic."

"We have a friendly to your 9 o'clock."

Nehemiah heard her voice before all hell broke loose and shots rang out.

Nehemiah sat straight up in bed, drenched in a full sweat. Like every other night, the terrors woke him up at the same moment in the dream. He relived that tragic event, night after night. Why him? Why her? He always questioned himself. Nothing could change the past, but the dreams continued to come.

Like clockwork, he went into the kitchen of his one-bedroom apartment in Portsmouth, VA and grabbed a beer from the refrigerator. He sat in front of his television, but never turned it on. Nehemiah wanted to close his eyes, but every time he did, he saw her face, her eyes, and her blood.

Draining the contents of the bottle, he went back into his bedroom and sat on the edge of the bed. Face to palms, he sat there for a few minutes, feeling weary.

"Come back to bed. It's cold under these sheets," a soft feminine voice said.

Nehemiah needed to stop all of this philandering he was doing. His actions went against every principle and every value he was raised with.

"I'll be right there," he responded.

What was her name? He couldn't remember her name or where he met her. Yeah, it was time to change his lifestyle.

2 Years Later

"Where are you headed to for your leave?" Master Chief Petty Officer McEntire asked. Peter McEntire, also known as, Mac, or by his code name, Civic, was the commanding officer of their military unit. A naval unit covertly assembled to see things and not be seen. Unlike the Navy Seals or Army Rangers, their unit had no name, and no one outside of the Commander of Naval Operations and the Director of Defense Intelligence knew they existed.

"Master Chief, I'm headed to San Juan for some relaxation. What about you? Any big plans?" Nehemiah asked.

"Nah, just spending quality time with Riolo." Riolo was his German Shepherd and best friend. Mac rescued the dog from a frigid pond in northern Michigan one winter, and the two have been inseparable ever since. Nehemiah often wondered if the reason the Master Chief wasn't married was due to his job or his insane love affair with his dog.

Later that day, Nehemiah was in his sparsely filled apartment packing the last of his gear and heading for the airport. He kept an apartment in Portsmouth, VA as a landing pad, only using it when he was in Virginia for work or visiting with his parents. There was no need to have anything other than a bed and television in his apartment since he never invited people over, except for the occasional woman to entertain.

He was looking forward to two weeks of beach and drinks. This vacation was what he needed. The stress of his life was beginning to take a toll on him. His last assignment had him re-evaluating the important things in life. Nehemiah knew being in the military was temporary; in fact, he had recently been contemplating retirement. Aside from being a career military man like his father, Nehemiah also had investments in his brother's recording studio, and he had started a security firm with offices in northern Virginia and Florida.

The security firm was his next great challenge. He hired only ex-military and law enforcement personnel, men and women he knew that could handle themselves under intense pressure. Their backgrounds had to be clean and perfect before Nehemiah would invite an applicant for an interview.

Jake Lewis ran the day-to-day operations of Divine Security and Protection Services. They met at Great Lakes Recruit Training and had been close friends ever since. Jake stayed enlisted for 12 years before he was medically discharged due to a leg injury that he suffered. He liked to tell people it was a combat mission, but he was accidentally hit with a metal pipe doing some routine maintenance.

After only being in business for a year, they had a decent clientele list thanks to Nehemiah's youngest brother, Elijah, also known as, mega pop-star, Evolution. He had introduced them to many entertainers and athletes who were always in need of bodyguards or extra security for one reason or another. Nehemiah and Jake also dabbled in investigations. Though, not the bulk of their business, they were intrigued by the adrenaline rush they would get after solving a mystery; even if the mystery was spying on cheating spouses.

Nehemiah scheduled a flight layover in Washington, D.C. to check on things in the office before he continued to Puerto Rico. He flew into Ronald Reagan National Airport and caught a cab to his small office near the Fashion Centre at Pentagon City. The office was quiet for a weekday. He expected to see Jake or at least his administrative assistant. The office door was unlocked, so someone must have been inside.

"Hello? Is anyone here?" Nehemiah yelled. He heard bumping coming from the utility room in the rear of the office. "Come out now! I'm armed, and I won't ask again." This time, he yelled with a deadly chill to his voice.

"Man, you're not armed," Jake said coming out of the room zipping his pants. "I know better than that."

Before Nehemiah could question Jake, his assistant exited the room adjusting her clothing. She didn't bother to look ashamed. She quietly walked past them and gave Jake a naughty look.

"You couldn't call before you stopped by?" Jake walked into his office with Nehemiah following behind him.

"I don't need to call. Remember I own half of this business?" he said taking a seat in front of Jake's desk while Jake went into the attached bathroom to freshen up. "Besides, the door was unlocked. What if I were a client or potential client and walked in here to find you and the receptionist in the closet?"

"That's not the norm. Besides, she needed some help getting some copy paper from the top shelf, and then one thing led to another," Jake laughed. He left the bathroom, closed his office door, then took a seat behind his desk.

"Whatever, Jake. Don't let it happen, again. And what happened to the other assistant you had? You know the one with the big…"

"Yeah, Barbara or Brenda…whatever her name was. She didn't work out," Jake laughed again at his inside joke. "This one is working out great."

Nehemiah thought she was working out great for Jake alright. Beautiful women were the one thing he and Jake had in common. Except now, Nehemiah was growing tired of multiple women. His mother admonished him every time he brought a different woman around the family.

That had him thinking about retirement again, and settling down with one woman, and possibly starting a family. His oldest brother, Aaron, was married with four children, his sisters Naomi and Ruth were both married with three children each. He also had two younger brothers and a younger sister who were all happily single.

"I stopped by to check on you and the office."

"Cut the crap. You know what's been going on around here. I know you get the monthly reports," Jake stated. "But I can tell you, I just contracted with Senator Greenhouse of Texas. Apparently, there are a few women's groups that don't particularly care for his stance on women's issues. While in D.C., he wants additional security."

Nehemiah stretched out his long legs and propped them up on Jake's desk. "Tell me about this other new case?" The monthly report mentioned a possible new case with the federal government.

"Nothing much to tell so far. It's just surveillance." Leaning forward, Jake asked, "Where did you say you were going on vacation?"

"Puerto Rico. Why?"

"Planning to stay on the beach? In, say, one of those fancy resorts?"

"What are you getting at Jake? Just spit it out."

"Keep your eyes and ears open while you're down there. The new job mentioned San Juan. I'm sending two of our guys down there tomorrow. They'll be staying at different resorts on opposite ends of the beach. Remember, it's just surveillance."

The surveillance case involved a drug cartel, child trafficking, and money laundering. While Nehemiah was relaxing, he could keep his eyes open for any shadiness happening around him. They talked for a few more minutes about a couple of other clients and possibly a new investigative case involving a runaway rich kid.

Nehemiah had reservations about taking the surveillance case at first. Drug cartels were best left to the federal government. The feds had more resources and the ability to travel and operate internationally. However, they did need more clients, and the fees that would come along with this case would help to expand and possibly be able to offer full-time employment to some of their guys. As it was now, all the security guys they hired were contractors.

Hopefully, with the increase in clients Divine Protection would allow Nehemiah to fully retire and settle down. Maybe an exit from this life would help to get rid of the nightmares.

San Juan, Puerto Rico was a beautiful place. Nehemiah was planning to stay at a beach resort in Condado. Rest and relaxation were on the menu, as well as, visiting a few casinos while he was there. He entered the hotel lobby causing quite a stir. His towering 6'8" height and powerful physique were known to cause a light ruckus among women. He was wearing a sleeveless t-shirt and cargo shorts showing off his muscular arms and well-toned legs. He tried to disappear behind a baseball cap and a pair of sunglasses, but that didn't seem to work.

The stares and whispers from women took some time getting used to, but Nehemiah accepted that it went with the territory. Usually, he ignored the subtle and blatant attempts by women to get his attention. Most women thought he was a professional athlete and he never confirmed nor denied their assumptions. He let them believe what they wanted.

Over the years, he watched his youngest brother, Elijah, deal with crazy and eccentric fans. Women would do some of the most outlandish things just to touch the pop-star, or to get a piece of his clothing. Since the women in the hotel lobby were just looking, Nehemiah figured if he kept his attention focused straight ahead, a few stares wouldn't kill him.

He was able to check into his hotel room without causing too much trouble. Only one woman was bold enough to make a pass at him, which he quickly turned down. In the past, he would have invited the woman to his room for a rendezvous, but this time, he really wanted and needed the solitude.

There was a change happening within him, and Nehemiah was ready to make the change. He no longer had the desire to spend time with multiple women, and he was beginning to crave what his parents had, a stable home and a family.

Day 1

His room was very spacious with separate sitting and bedroom areas. The bedroom had an excellent view of the beach and ocean. He was located on the fourth floor and had a large outside balcony with a table and two chairs. The deck also had a jacuzzi hot tub, which Nehemiah knew he would be using in the very near future. The balcony for the room next door was separated by a frosted glass partition.

After checking out his room, Nehemiah decided to take a hot shower and then try out the massage therapist in the resort's spa. After his shower, he dressed very casually in another pair of cargo shorts and a *Virginia Beach is for Lovers* T-shirt. On the way to the spa, he was doing his best to ignore the lustful looks of women as he passed them. One woman openly gawked at him on the elevator. He kept his head low and didn't make eye contact. Until he unintentionally knocked down a petite woman wearing a housekeeping uniform.

"Excuse me, *Señor*. I was not paying attention," she said, attempting to stand.

Nehemiah reached for her hands to help her up. He immediately noticed how soft and small her hands were. Looking into her eyes, he saw fear. He wasn't ready for the despair he saw in her face. Her eyes, the look she gave him, gut-punched him, and he immediately felt a strange sensation and didn't know what to make of it.

"*Señorita, por favor, fue mi culpa*," Nehemiah responded in Spanish that it was his fault.

With wide eyes, she asked, "*¿hablas español?*"

"*Un poco*," he replied, giving her his killer smile that was known for causing women to melt.

Instead of returning his smile, she frowned, averted her eyes and excused herself before turning around and running away.

There was a first for everything. Nehemiah had never had a woman run away from him. Usually, they flocked to him. Instead of dwelling on what just happened, he shook his head and continued to the spa.

After an intense hour-long Swedish massage, Nehemiah relaxed on the balcony of his room, enjoying the sun and solitude. He was lost in his thoughts, and as much as he tried not to think of that horrible night two years ago, his memory would take over. He stressed over how he could have done things differently or what signs he had missed.

He didn't like to keep reliving that moment over again. This was the part of post-traumatic stress disorder he couldn't seem to shake. He did the required counseling sessions after a mission, but this particular mission and its outcome, was causing Nehemiah to rethink his career choice. One bad decision changed the trajectory of his life.

Breaking him free from his misery was the sound of a door opening. "Housekeeping."

The voice sounded far away, he wasn't sure if the housekeeper was entering his room or the room next door. Taking a towel from the table next to him, he wiped the moisture from his brow and opened the sliding glass door, startling the housekeeper as she entered.

"I'm sorry, *Señor*, I thought you were out for the day," she said.

Nehemiah realized it was her again. The housekeeper he had knocked down earlier in the day. She had bowed her head, avoiding direct eye contact and tried to back out of the room. He scanned her body from head to toe and landed on a bruise on her right bicep.

"I'm so sorry. I didn't mean to hurt you."

"*Señor*? You didn't hurt me." She appeared confused until she looked down at her arm and saw the bruise. She tried to cover it with the sleeve of her uniform. Nervously she said, "I will come back later."

Before Nehemiah could respond, she was out the door. He wondered what that was about. If the bruise had not been from her fall, then where did it come from? He took a real good look at her when he helped her up, and he didn't remember seeing the bruise.

He thought about his great-aunt who always had bruises after leaving the casino. The family teased her that she would get these bruises from hitting the slot machines when she was losing, and that was pretty much all the time. Maybe her bruise was innocent.

Laughing at the thought of his aunt, Nehemiah returned to the balcony to continue relaxing. Tomorrow, he would check out the beach and take in a neighborhood restaurant. The cuisine from the local places was always better than the food in the resorts.

"Angel, come in."

"Go, Civic."

"We have a friendly to your 9 o'clock."

Nehemiah heard her voice, but it couldn't be her. He searched the smoky room, trying to find the person talking. His eyes landed on her the minute the gun was pointed toward her head.

Nehemiah jumped awake, not knowing where he was, and slammed his body to the floor, taking the chair with him.

"Yo, man, you alright over there?" a guy from the room next to his asked.

He realized he was still on the balcony of the resort. He must have fallen asleep out there. The sky was a hazy rust color as the sun was setting.

"Yea, I'm okay. Thanks." Nehemiah responded. He stood and righted the chair before returning into his room. He couldn't go back to sleep, so he decided on a cup of coffee and some television. The memories were too much for him to handle. Even after two years, he could still see everything vividly.

Day 2

Nehemiah was awake at the crack of dawn preparing for his ritual, early morning work-out. He kept his body in tip-top shape by doing basic exercises of 300 push-ups & sit-ups every morning, then going for a five to six-mile jog. When at home or on the base, he would include a lot more strength training into his daily workout. While on vacation, he decided to keep his routine light.

His run took him through the neighborhood of Old San Juan. The streets reminded him of Italy. They were narrow, and sidewalks were non-existent. Nehemiah took a break at the Castillo San Felipe del Morro, a 16th-century citadel located on the San Juan Bay. The citadel was designed to guard the bay and defend the port city of San Juan against seaborne enemies.

The morning air and solitude of his surroundings was the brief escape Nehemiah needed to relax his mind and forget the memories that kept him awake last night. His fitness tracker logged him at just over three miles from his hotel. He wanted to get back before the bustle of locals began. He took a quick drink from his water bottle and turned around to return to the resort.

Nehemiah was slowing his pace as he approached the resort. He checked his watch and noticed it was breakfast time. Which meant the lobby area leading to the restaurant would be crowded. Not wanting to be seen or cause a stir of any kind, he jogged around to the back of the resort, to the employee entrance. None of the employees seemed to mind or care that he was not a hotel employee. They continued to work around him. Nehemiah was able to slip in and go straight to the guest elevators.

Day two of his vacation, and he wanted to check out the pool and, then, the beach. He was more relaxed than the day before, and his early morning workout helped. He grabbed a lounge chair near the pool-side bar, discarded his t-shirt and flip flops and dived into the deep end of the pool.

Being in the water was second nature to Nehemiah. He was a championship high school swimmer and track-star. He wanted to play football when he was younger, but his mother forbade it. She only allowed non-contact sports. She would go crazy if she knew just how physical a game of basketball could get, especially among the Bolden children. The girls were just as physical when it came to family competitiveness. And, the Bolden children could make anything a competition.

All of his siblings had been athletic in school. Aaron and Moses were stand-out basketball players. Naomi was all-American in volleyball and softball, Ruth ran cross-country track, Rachel shared Nehemiah's love of swimming, and Elijah was into soccer. That was until he discovered music and girls.

Nehemiah was the third oldest son, and middle child of seven children to Jaclyn and Jeremiah Bolden. Aaron, Ruth, and Moses were the oldest, and then, Naomi, Rachel, and his baby brother Elijah. They had grown up navy brats, traveling the world with their father. Only Nehemiah followed in his father's footsteps and joined the military.

After a few laps in the pool, Nehemiah noticed that he was beginning to draw unwanted female attention and decided it was time to try another activity...maybe jet-skis. He was hoping he could make it to his lounge chair, grab a drink of water and head to the beach without being stopped. No such luck.

"Do I know you?" a beautiful blonde woman asked him.

"I don't think so," Nehemiah tried to dismiss her and stepped around her.

She moved back in front him, blocking his access to his lounge chair. "You look so familiar to me. Hi, I'm Summer." She held out her hand for him to shake.

He didn't want to be rude, so he accepted her hand. She used that moment to her advantage by pulling herself closer.

"I'm in room 1722. Stop by later." She released his hand and walked away.

Nehemiah shook his head in disgust and gathered his belongings. He overheard the bartender say, "That never happens to me."

"I wish it didn't happen to me," Nehemiah replied, and walked down the boardwalk to the beach area.

The sea breeze was a pleasant break from the chlorine smell of the pool. Nehemiah preferred swimming in pools and going on adventures in the ocean. He rented a jet ski for an hour, and then, did a little snorkeling before meeting up with some guys he had met who were renting a boat to do some deep-sea diving. By the time he returned to the resort, he was ready for a midday siesta.

Heading straight for his room he noticed the housekeeping cart was in front of his door. Maybe he would get to see the cleaning lady he had accidentally knocked over. As luck would have it, she was backing out of his room as he was entering.

"It seems we keep meeting like this," he said in his ultra-sexy baritone voice.

She jumped at the sound of his voice. "Señor, you must stop scaring me like this." Bowing her head, she rushed to her cart and pushed it to the next set of room doors.

He wasn't going to let her just walk away this time. "My name is Nehemiah. What's your name?"

"My name? Why?"

That was a good question. Why was he asking for her name? What was he planning to do with that information? "I thought it would be common courtesy to tell you my name since you have been cleaning my room," he said, when he couldn't think of anything else. This was a first for him. He had never been tongue-tied around a woman before. He was a little unsure of himself.

She raised an eyebrow at him, giving him a once over before answering. "My name is Gabriella."

"See that wasn't so difficult. It was a pleasure to meet you, Gabriella. Have a nice day." He gave her his signature smile and was about to enter his room when he noticed a bruise on her left leg. "Gabriella, are you okay? You have another bruise."

She looked down at her leg and then scurried to the other side of her cleaning cart. "It must have happened yesterday. I fell mopping my kitchen floor." She looked embarrassed and quickly entered the next room to clean.

Nehemiah felt something wasn't right. A bruise on her arm and now a deep purple bruise on her left leg. He wasn't getting a good feeling about this one. He entered his room and tried to shake it off by grabbing a beer from the mini-fridge, but something kept bringing him back to Gabriella. The look in her eyes begged for help; and he felt that strange sensation again. He wouldn't be satisfied until he found out what was going on with her.

Day 3

Nehemiah decided after his morning run, he would make his way to the market. He wanted to pick up some gifts for his nieces and nephews. Even though Aaron's children were well-traveled, they still loved and appreciated gifts from Uncle Miah.

He strolled the crowded market looking for the right items. Trying to decide between a shell necklace or a straw purse for his niece, Mariah, he heard a commotion from the other side of the market. His Spanish was very limited, but he was able to make out the words: *stop, please,* and *no.* He looked toward the commotion, and there was Gabriella; only this time she was with a man. The man was much bigger than her, and he had a death grip on her arm. He was dragging her through the market while she screamed. People looked, but no one seemed to want to help her.

Nehemiah was not about to let this happen. He tried to approach her but was stopped by an elderly woman who shook her head at him. He wasn't raised to ignore someone in need, so he went around the old woman.

"Hey, what's going on over here?" Nehemiah used his deep, lethal voice to gain their attention.

"*No, Señor, por favor,*" Gabriella pleaded with him. Her eyes were saying "*help me,*" but she was verbally telling him to stay away.

"Who the hell is this guy? Are you screwing him?" the man yelled at her and refused to release the death grip he had on her arm.

Nehemiah was getting angry but wouldn't let it show. Due to years of training, he had the ability to remain calm in the harshest situations.

In a slow even tone, Nehemiah said, "Sir, please do not continue to cause a scene. The lady does not want to go with you. Just let her go."

"Sure, she wants to come with me. Don't you, honey? This is my wife; she has to come with me." He jerked her close to him, again.

"Gabriella, you do not have to go with him," Nehemiah tried to tell her.

"*Señor,* this is my husband. I must go with him." Her eyes pleaded with him, but she continued to be dragged away. Her husband pushed her into a waiting vehicle and sped away.

Nehemiah wasn't sure why he felt the need to get involved. He stood there watching the vehicle drive away, unable to help a woman he knew for sure wanted help. The people in the market seemed to go about their business as if nothing happened. Unbelievable that no one tried to help her.

The elderly woman who tried to stop him from getting involved approached him. "Sometimes, you can't help those who don't know they can be helped." She paused to make sure Nehemiah was looking at her. "If you really want to help her, go to Inferno."

Nehemiah thought about what the lady had said as he finished shopping. He continued to think about it as he walked back to the resort. Did Gabriella know there was help out there for her? Did she want the help her eyes so desperately communicated? And, what was Inferno?

Still, in thought, he absently walked through the front lobby of his resort and was almost immediately accosted by the blonde woman from the pool the previous day. Today she was wearing a different 2-piece swimsuit with a see-through sarong tied across her slim hips.

"I missed you last night. You didn't stop by," she said, in an annoying whine. He assumed the pout she was giving him was supposed to make him feel bad for not taking her up on her offer.

"I had other things to do. Enjoy your day." He tried to side-step her, but she moved back in front of him. "Well, we're having a party tonight in my suite. Room 1722. I will excuse your bad manners if you join us."

Nehemiah was frustrated, and with so many other things on his mind, he tried not to sound rude when he responded, "I don't know you, and I will not be coming to your suite tonight or any other night." He left her standing there infuriated.

Instead of going straight to his room, he stopped by the concierge desk. "*Señor*, how may I help you?"

"What is Inferno?" Nehemiah asked in a hushed tone.

"Inferno is a dance club on the other side of the island. I do not recommend you go there."

"And, why is that?"

"It is not known to be safe. For tourists or locals."

"Great. Give me the address."

The concierge looked reluctant to give him the address. Nehemiah's dark, piercing stare made the man tremble and immediately write the address on a piece of paper. With the address in hand, Nehemiah returned to his suite to see if he could pull together something to wear. He had no intentions of partying, so he didn't bring any party clothes.

His father, Jeremiah Bolden's famous saying, "Be prepared for anything," must have still been lingering in the back of Nehemiah's mind. He had packed a pair of black slacks and a black button up. Unfortunately, he needed to purchase a pair of new shoes. His sisters were always saying that one could never have too many shoes, but he didn't believe in that philosophy. Nehemiah figured if he didn't need the shoes after tonight, he would donate them when he got home.

By 10:00pm, Nehemiah was dressed to kill. He hired a driver so he wouldn't have to wait on a cab when he was ready to leave. This wasn't just a night on the town. He had a feeling he was about to step into something he wouldn't easily get out of. The car pulled up in front of an empty warehouse. There were a few cars outside, but no people anywhere.

"Are you sure this is the right place?"

"You asked for Inferno, *sí?*

"*Sí*, but this is an empty building."

"Ah, looks can be deceiving my friend."

Nehemiah instructed the driver to stay close before exiting the vehicle. Observing his surroundings, he noticed a security camera atop of the building and a glint of light caught his attention from the roof. It looked to be an armed gunman up there. Without noticing anything else suspicious outside, he approached the side door to the building. He knocked a few times, and then waited.

A burly man strapped with a .38 caliber gun on his side opened the door wide enough for a much smaller man to come out. He motioned for Nehemiah to lift his arms and proceeded to pat him down, checking for weapons. These guys didn't know that Nehemiah was a trained mercenary. He could disarm both men without making a sound. Once the man finished, the smaller man nodded his head toward the entrance.

Nehemiah paid $50 to enter; and inside was a stark contrast to the outside. The Inferno was a lively nightclub. A dance floor in the center of the room was filled to capacity. He wondered where these people parked their cars, or if everyone took a cab. He quickly scanned the room and noticed three exits and a handful of armed gunmen. Two of the gunmen were guarding an area just to the right of the dance floor.

It was difficult to maneuver around without bumping into someone dancing and gyrating about the floor. He finally made it to the bar and was able to snag a stool just as a man was being led to the dance floor by a scantily dressed and very young-looking girl. Nehemiah ordered a Don Q with cranberry juice and continued to check out the place.

After about an hour of sipping on his drink, the hairs on the back of his neck stood on end. Something didn't feel right. He scanned the place, trying to find what that something was, when his eyes deceived him. Sitting in the large VIP area near the dance floor was a man he knew for sure was dead. Immediately, Nehemiah's past slapped him across the face. Carlos Ortiz, drug trafficker, was killed years ago.

Tossing back his drink, he threw a $100 bill on the bar and started to leave. But then he saw Gabriella's husband enter the VIP area. This was no coincidence. The old woman from the market knew he would be there for Nehemiah to see. He wondered if she knew about his involvement with Ortiz too.

Quickly, Nehemiah exited the building and jumped back into his car.

"Did you not find what you were looking for?" the driver asked.

"That, and more. Back to the resort, please."

Nehemiah sat in the back seat, recovering from the shock of what he had just witnessed as he texted his Master Chief.

Mac...just saw Ortiz w/ my own eyes

No way. He's dead
Or so we thought...

Back in his room, Nehemiah called Jake. He needed to know more about the observation assignment. Manuel Ortiz was a drug trafficker that was killed over three years ago by Nehemiah's team. It was impossible that he survived that attack. "Dude, you gotta wake up."

"I'm up. Where's the fire?" Jake replied.

"Tell me more about this new client, and what do you know about the drug trafficking in San Juan?"

"Damn, dude, I said you only needed to observe. What have you gotten yourself into?"

Pacing the floor, Nehemiah replied, "I just saw a ghost. I need to know everything about the case."

Jake went over everything in the case folder that was provided to him. The Federal Bureau of Investigations had hired them, and the case was supposed to be simple surveillance. Leave it to Nehemiah to make it more than that. The F.B.I. rarely used outside security teams to do this type of work, and that also confused Nehemiah. He continued to pace his room, thinking. Not sure what to make of the events of the night. Now, more than anything, he needed to find Gabriella and figure out what was going on. What had he gotten himself into?

Day 4

Nehemiah was barely able to sleep through the night. Memories of that night continued to flood his mind. And, Jake was taking his time getting back to him with additional information about the case. He didn't want to leave his hotel room in hopes of seeing Gabriella. Hopefully, she would be his housekeeper again today. She could possibly answer questions that he had about what was going on.

Instead of his usual morning workout, Nehemiah decided to do some research of his own. He opened his tablet and tried to search for any information on Manuel Ortiz. Google wasn't very forthcoming, but he did access a private security system run by the Department of Defense.

Unfortunately, he was unable to find out anything about Ortiz, and he didn't have a name for Gabriella's husband. Nehemiah was becoming increasingly frustrated with the lack of information, but he knew he was there on that island and at that specific resort for a reason. God didn't make mistakes, as his mother always said.

The ringing of his cell phone brought him out of his thoughts. He quickly scanned the caller ID and answered when he saw it was Jake finally calling him back.

"Jake, tell me something good."

"Really. Does trouble come looking for you everywhere you go? I've been on every government site I could find last night, and I found some drug trafficking and some sex-trafficking going on in the area. Let's start with the drugs. Appears they are coming over from Central America and making its way by boat to Puerto Rico. The crazy thing is, those drugs may be coming in by way of the naval base there."

"Roosevelt Roads Naval Station was closed in 2004."

"The local reserve units still run military drills there," Jake informed him. "There's more. Homeland Security is currently monitoring a group for trafficking children. They are grabbing young girls from hotel resorts just like the one where you are staying. In the past six months, three girls have come up missing from your resort. Two from the resort next door, and three from a few hotels down the beach. A total of eight girls in six months. Mostly Puerto Rican teenagers; and the police are calling them runaways and not abductions."

"Damnit! Ok, I think this housekeeper here at the hotel may know something. I saw her husband with Ortiz at a night club last night."

"What makes you think she knows anything? And, why are you getting involved? This is supposed to be surveillance."

That was the question of the hour. Why was he getting involved? Nehemiah didn't have a good answer for that. An uneasiness had settled in the pit of his stomach. He knew something wasn't adding up, and he felt Gabriella was in the center of it.

The two men talked more about the drug trafficking and how the drugs were coming through the base. The only possible way was there had to be an inside man. Someone who was turning the other way when deliveries were being made.

Nehemiah waited for housekeeping to show up in hopes it would be Gabriella. When the knock on the door came, it was not her. He tried to ask the friendly older lady about Gabriella, but she wouldn't respond. Nehemiah knew the woman understood his limited Spanish. She made a small twitch with her smile when he mentioned Gabriella's name.

Since waiting for her was a bust, he thought about going back to the market to visit the old lady. Maybe she was some type of psychic, but even that sounded crazy to him. He had not eaten since he had room service bring him breakfast, so Nehemiah headed to the bar located in the lobby of his hotel. He was thinking about the girls that had gone missing in the past months. Not one mention of them on the news.

Searching through his smartphone, he tried to find any news articles about kidnappings or even runaways from San Juan; and there was nothing. He remembered Jake saying most of the girls were Puerto Rican. He sent a text message to Jake asking about the nationality of the other girls. The reply came immediately; one missing girl was Haitian, and the other was a teenager from Panama. Both were from poor families seeking a better life in Puerto Rico.

Nehemiah needed answers. The feeling in his gut was telling him there was more, again. He had more questions and hoped his commanding officer would have some answers. He was just about to call Mac when he saw Gabriella through the mirror behind the bar, rushing into the hotel. She was keeping her head down but had looked up to glance around. Nehemiah followed her through the employee-only doors and into, what appeared to be, a staff locker room.

"Gabriella?" She jumped at the sound of his voice. "I didn't mean to scare you."

"*Señor*, you cannot be here. You must leave," she told him.

Nehemiah stood tall and didn't move. He stared at her from head to toe until he finally noticed the amount of makeup on her face. He went to reach for her chin, and she flinched and cowered.

"I'm sorry. I won't hurt you."

"They always say that. Please, leave me alone. It will be better for all of us."

"Sorry about that, too, but I cannot leave. Please, let me see your face."

Gabriella hesitated before lifting her face to him. He immediately saw a bruise to her right cheek and the darkening circle around her eyes.

In a menacing voice that initially caused Gabriella to shiver, Nehemiah stated, "He beats you." He didn't need to ask the question, the evidence was on her face, arms, and legs. The bruises he thought he caused due to the fall were from her husband. A man who was supposed to love her.

"Listen, he has eyes everywhere. He knows everything. *Señor*, I have a daughter at home. He will hurt her," she cried.

"Gabriella, I can help you and your daughter. I promise I can," he tried to assure her.

"No, no, no. No one can help. The police, the government. they all say, but no one helps." She grabbed her uniform from her locker and walked away.

"If you want my help, my room could use some fresh towels." He said to her retreating back. He hoped she would return.

Day 5

Nehemiah waited around his hotel for hours the day before. Hoping that Gabriella would come. He wanted to help her, wanted to keep her safe. The need to do something was overwhelming and nearly obsessive. No matter what the circumstance, he would not just leave, knowing he had the means to get her out of this life of violence.

He went for his morning jog and, again, ended up in the market. Only a few of the vendors were preparing their space for the day. Nehemiah was looking for the elderly lady to find out anything more dealing with Gabriella. He was preparing to leave and come back later when he spotted the lady. Or rather, she spotted him. She slightly motioned for him to follow her and she disappeared behind some tall shade trees. He kept his distance away from her but continued to follow her up a winding path behind a dilapidated house.

"You come here looking for me?"

"Yes, Ma'am. I need to know what else you know about the lady from the other day...Gabriella?"

"*Si*, Gabriella," she smiled. "First, you carry these boxes to the market for me."

Nehemiah instantly grabbed the boxes and followed the lady back to the market. He waited for her to say something more, but she didn't. She pulled a cart down the path until they arrived at her table within the market. He assisted her, and then, waited while she finished setting up her entire booth.

He could tell she was a beauty in her youth. Her straight black hair was long and stopped near her waist. Her eyes had seen better days, but still held a fire that was full of energy. Every so often, she would look up and smile. The only indication that she remembered Nehemiah was still standing there.

The elderly lady motioned for him to bend down to her level, grabbing both sides of his face with her weathered hands, she kissed him on the cheek and told him, "You have everything you need to know." She, then, dismissed him with the flick of her wrist and continued preparing for her day.

He had just wasted at least 45 minutes helping this woman prepare for the market, and she did not share anything with him that he could use to find Gabriella. He wanted to ask her a question about Inferno, or at least find out Gabriella's last name. He looked around. The market was packed, and the lady was busy with her customers.

Instead of waiting any longer, Nehemiah jogged back to the resort planning to take a shower and look for Gabriella once again. He went to undress and felt something in the pockets of his gym shorts. The paper was a hand-written note in Spanish but addressed to Gabriella. The old lady must have slipped it into his pockets at some point. He didn't notice her do that, and that disturbed him.

Now determined more than ever, Nehemiah showered quickly, dressed and was heading out of the room when the bedside phone began ringing. The only people who knew where he was staying was Jake and Mac.

"Yeah?"

"This is Jake. I couldn't get through on your cell phone, so I thought I would try the room."

"My cell phone is around here somewhere," he said, looking around the room.

"Something crazy is going on. I picked up some weird chatter talking about you. Someone there knows who you are, and they are watching you. Be careful. I'm sending you back-up."

"Thanks, Jake. I owe you big."

"Yes, you do. Oh, and another thing. Mac has been looking for you, too. I think he is on his way to the island."

Great! That was all Nehemiah needed...to be working while he was on vacation, but wasn't that exactly what he was doing now... working? He was just about to start looking for his cell phone when there was a knock at the door. "Housekeeping."

He waited for a second to see if she would use her key, and she didn't. She knocked, again. "You asked for towels."

Nehemiah opened the door and was shocked to see Gabriella and a little girl who must have been her daughter. She rushed inside as soon as he opened the door and immediately closed it behind her. There was fear in her eyes, but she was standing strong. He admired that about her. She decided to take her life back.

"This is my daughter, Tiffany. You said you want to help? Start here. Keep her safe. The market lady said I could trust you. She gave me this letter for you." She turned to her daughter. "*Mija*, this man will take care of you until I return. Don't cry. He has cable." She stood and addressed Nehemiah again. "She is quiet and likes TV. She will eat anything. I will return soon." Gabriella started for the door.

"Wait! I have something for you." Nehemiah went to the nightstand and retrieved the letter the old lady had given to him for her.

He could see she was still afraid. She accepted the letter and smiled for the first time before leaving.

Nehemiah turned to the little girl who didn't appear too afraid. She stood in place, not moving, and clutching a doll who had seen better days. She was also carrying a backpack that seemed to be stuffed.

"Hello, Tiffany. My name is Nehemiah, but I let my friends call me, Miah. How old are you?"

Hesitant to speak, she eventually whispered, "I'm five years old."

"Wow, five. That's amazing. Would you like to watch television?"

She bobbed her head up and down with the most dazzling smile that was so much like her mother. He had her sit on the sofa in the sitting area of his room and ordered her a cartoon movie from the hotel movie selection.

Now, he was really in trouble. He realized the situation was getting out of control. He wasn't expecting to take in the woman or care for her child, but now that he offered, he couldn't turn his back on her. And, she could still possibly have information on Ortiz.

After getting Tiffany situated on the sofa, Nehemiah sat in a chair across from the girl and opened the letter Gabriella gave to him. The older lady had written a quick note instructing him to take Gabriella off the island and keep her safe. She didn't deserve all the things that have happened in her life. She needed a fresh start.

Nehemiah finally found his cell phone and remembered the ringer had been turned off. He noticed he had five missed calls and three text messages...all from Mac, who was indeed, on his way to the resort. He had landed over an hour ago. Nehemiah quickly texted his room number to his C.O. and patiently waited for him to arrive.

It only took fifteen minutes before Mac was beating on his door. Nehemiah noticed that Tiffany had jumped at the knocking, and she instantly curled into the fetal position. His heart ached for the little girl who had probably seen more than she should have at her age.

"Tiffany, it's okay. It's a friend of mine," Nehemiah tried to console the girl. He turned to the door and opened it before Mac could start pounding again.

"What the hell took you so long...?"

"Shh! Language." Nehemiah pointed to the frightened girl on the sofa.

"Who is that?" he whispered.

"That is Gabriella's daughter. She dropped her off about twenty minutes ago."

"Well, who is Gabriella?"

"Come on, let's go in the other room and talk." Nehemiah smiled at Tiffany and winked, hoping to ease some of her fears. He didn't completely close the door, wanting to make sure he still had eyes on Tiffany. "Listen, I met this housekeeper here at the resort. She is in an abusive relationship. I wanted to help her and then found out her husband is tied up with Ortiz somehow."

Mac handed him the top-secret file on Ortiz. "It seems as though you did see Ortiz in the club. His body was never recovered after the incident."

Nehemiah took the file and started reviewing the documents. *How could he be alive? How could anyone survive that attack?*

"Don't do it, Bolden. He may have survived, but she didn't."

Nehemiah couldn't help thinking about her. Chrystal Bell, whose code name was Silver, was a CIA special operative. She was killed in action working on a case with Nehemiah's team. For two years, she was embedded in his unit. And, for two years, no one knew that they were involved in a relationship. They tried to deny their attraction to one another, but after only a few weeks in denial, they reacted to the passion sizzling between them.

She had been killed during an attack on Ortiz in Panama. The intelligence was good, and the mission should have been textbook. Yet, things went wrong, a counter assault happened, and people were killed, including Silver.

The door opening in the other room caused both men to be on alert. Quickly, Nehemiah swooped into the sitting area and grabbed Tiffany, taking her to the floor and covering her mouth so she didn't scream.

"Señor? It's Gabriella." She came further into the room and saw Mac standing with a gun to his side. She immediately froze in place and searched the room looking for her daughter.

Nehemiah saw the fear in her eyes and released Tiffany to go to her mother. He didn't want to scare her any further and he needed them both to trust him.

"Gabriella, this is a co-worker," he tried to explain.

Once Gabriella was able to recover her voice, she looked to both men, then asked Nehemiah, "Can he be trusted? Really trusted?"

"Yes," Nehemiah answered.

"Good. You said you want to help. Here we are."

"I don't understand," Mac said.

"This is all I have in this world; the clothes on my back and my daughter. We have nothing else. I left my husband. Once he finds out, he will be furious, and I will become a target. They will kill us. Can you take us to the states and hide us there?"

Nehemiah and Mac spent the next few hours contacting everyone they knew in the states to get some assistance. While they were doing that, Gabriella explained to them that Ortiz was not only trafficking drugs, but also, children. Ortiz and her husband, Carlos Montoya, threatened her if she ever said anything about what she knew. They promised they would take Tiffany from her, so she remained quiet. Gabriella told them she had proof of the illegal activities but would only share it when she and her daughter were safe stateside.

Nehemiah, Gabriella, Tiffany, and Mac switched hotels and checked in under assumed names. Changing hotels was necessary to move undetected as much as possible. Someone on the island had identified Nehemiah as a government employee which was akin to putting a bullseye on his back for the underworld to target him.

The back-up that Jake sent had been covert and unable to find out anything about the people who had identified Nehemiah in the first place. The daily chatter had been calm, and they all knew what that meant, a storm was coming. That made Nehemiah nervous because he didn't know what to expect. Not knowing also made it difficult to protect Gabriella and Tiffany.

Nehemiah watched how Gabriella stayed observant, yet fearful at the same time. He also noticed how she had a natural beauty about her. He didn't ask her age, but he figured her to be about twenty-seven years old. She kept her hair pulled tightly atop her head, adding to her youthful appearance.

He had so many questions for her, but hadn't pressed for any information about her husband, Ortiz, or her involvement. She had willingly told them what she knew about the trafficking. Mac, on the other hand, wanted to interrogate her using his personal methods. Nehemiah had seen those methods and didn't like it at all.

He finally convinced Mac to let him take the lead. It wasn't an official case for Divine Protection, and it wasn't on the government's radar yet. In the meantime, he just wanted Gabriella to relax and learn to trust him.

They stayed in place for three days. Each day, they had their meals delivered by room service or a delivery service. All deliveries were checked by one of the guys Jake sent. By the third day, it was time to depart San Juan and head for safety. Nehemiah had been making plans for shelter and a job for Gabriella. He didn't want her venturing out alone, so he had to pull some strings to find her a stay- at-home job.

The apartment where she would be living belonged to one of his teammates. Patrick Holmes, also known as Pac-Man, rarely made it home to Indianapolis. He was the type of guy who didn't like to stay still for too long but needed a place of his own to stay when he visited family.

The morning they were scheduled to fly back stateside, Nehemiah, Gabriella, and Tiffany were leaving early, and through the employee entrance, so they were not seen, when they ran smack into the one person, he didn't need to see him.

"Nehemiah! What's up, Bro?" Elijah was being escorted to the service elevator by hotel security and his longtime bodyguard, Marco.

"Elijah, what are you doing here?" Nehemiah unsuccessfully tried to hide Gabriella behind him.

"Concert tonight, then some rest and relaxation. And, who do we have here?"

"This is Gabriella and Tiffany. I'm helping them out for a little while." Nehemiah looked around, "Where are Moses and Rachel?"

His older brother Moses, and younger sister Rachel, worked for Elijah and his companies in any capacity he needed them to. Rachel's official title was Public Relations Liaison, and Moses did anything that made life for his brother easier.

"Those two stopped to grab a bite to eat. You know how Rachel loves to eat."

"Right. Well, we have to get going."

"Okay, so when you get back, let's hang out. Come to the show tonight?"

"Actually, we're headed back stateside." Nehemiah continued to push Gabriella and Tiffany forward.

"I guess I'll see you back stateside," Elijah said

"Yeah, call me," Nehemiah moved them quickly out of the back door and into a waiting vehicle.

Nehemiah immediately called Jake once they were inside of the cab. He had to let him know that Elijah had seen them. His brother wouldn't be a problem and was someone he could trust, but he didn't want to get his family involved in any way.

Six hours later, the three of them landed safely in Indianapolis, Indiana. No one would think to look for them there. The apartment was already furnished, and the utilities were turned on. Nehemiah had someone do some grocery shopping for Gabriella, so her kitchen was fully stocked. He escorted her to the apartment and explained the part-time job working from home. She would be working as a virtual assistant for a company that a friend owned.

He was shocked to find out she had a business degree and was only a few credits short from getting her master's degree. Yet, she still had not said why she was working as a housekeeper for the resort. Nehemiah decided not to press her at this time.

"Nehemiah, I still do not understand. Why are you doing all of this for me? You were willing to help us even before you found out I had information on Ortiz. Why?"

He couldn't explain it, either. He just knew that this was something he had to do. Sure, he could have left her in San Juan, and he could have pumped her for more information about her husband and Ortiz, but he didn't. That was something he would have to do later.

For right now, he wanted to keep her safe until he needed her. She would become a witness in the federal cases against Manuel Ortiz and her husband, Carlos Montoya. Nehemiah was adamant about taking down the entire cartel and giving Gabriella her life back.

"All I can say is you needed help, and my mother would kill me if she found out I didn't do everything I could to help you."

"Are you going to stay here?" she said, fearfully.

"Just until tomorrow. You are safe here, I promise." He reassured her. "If it makes you feel better, I have written down all of my contact information. If you need me, you call. No matter what time it is." He, then, handed her a key ring with a silver dog tag attached. "This key is to my condo in Miami. If you ever feel unsafe and you can't reach me, go here. This tag has the address of the condo and my security code to get into the building."

Gabriella nodded her head in confirmation of what she was being told.

1 year later

Nehemiah hadn't been sleeping well. It had been three months since he last saw Gabriella. They had talked on the phone every night for the first month that she was in Indianapolis. He told himself it was to make sure she felt safe, but then he started visiting on weekends and anytime he had a few days off. He had fallen in love with Tiffany and, ultimately, her mother.

He didn't want to admit it, but he loved Gabriella more than he should. She was more complicated than he initially thought. She was educated and quite funny. She hadn't shared with him how she got mixed up with her husband, and he didn't want to know. He didn't want anything she did in her past to taint his thoughts of her.

Gabriella was a mystery to him. On the one hand, she was strong and almost dared someone to mess with her; and on the other hand, she sought shelter and protection from him. Even though he found comfort and love with Gabriella, the nightmares still haunted him. They occurred less frequently, and he thanked Gabriella for that. She was a quiet storm to his raging world.

Nehemiah wanted to visit her, even if for one night. Unfortunately, his unit was scheduled to ship out in a few days, and they had a lot of preparation to complete. Instead of visiting, he accepted that a phone call was all he would get. The phone rang a few times before she answered. Nehemiah replaced his usual greeting with, "Is everything okay?"

"Yes, of course. Why would you ask that?"

"Because, you didn't answer right away. I was getting concerned."

"There is no need to worry. I check in with Jake every night and every morning." They had established a security routine that had her checking in with Jake and having a security escort anytime she wanted to leave the apartment. She wasn't being held captive, but they needed to protect her. He needed to know she was protected.

She sounded nervous and hesitated when she spoke. He knew she wanted to say more. When she didn't speak up, he prompted her, "Gabriella, you can talk to me. About anything."

He heard her release her breath before dropping a bombshell on him, "I'm pregnant."

She said it so softly that Nehemiah was sure he misunderstood her. It wasn't possible that she said she was pregnant. His heart dropped to the floor. How could she do this to him? He was trying to protect her and keep her safe, and this is how she repaid him.

"Why?" Nehemiah could feel his heart ripping apart. He hadn't told her how he felt, but he hoped his actions were enough.

"Why? What do you mean why? I didn't do this on purpose," Gabriella started weeping, causing him to get angry. She didn't have a reason to cry. Her tears were wasted on him.

"Why are you telling me this? Did you tell the father?"

"You are the father."

Nehemiah dropped the phone from his hand. There was no way he messed up like that. He didn't make mistakes; he was always careful. The last time they were together was the first time they acted on the sexual passion that both had for one another. He had used a condom every time, he was sure of it.

Chapter 2

TODAY

There were four penthouse condos on the top floor of the building where the Bolden's lived. Their mother had prayed over and named each condo when Elijah first purchased them. Elijah and his wife, Karyn, occupied Condo Alpha full-time. Moses and his wife, Neiko, lived in Condo Calvary, and split their time between Miami and Atlanta. Rachel was single and lived alone in Condo Bathsheba. Condo Omega belonged to the rest of the family. Nehemiah usually occupied it when he was in town. On other occasions, other family members would stay there when visiting.

Karyn had just returned from taking her nephew Jaleel to school when she heard bumping coming from the unoccupied condo Omega. Moses and Neiko were in Atlanta, and Rachel should be in the office at this time of day. Karyn thought it would be best to contact building security, and then, she called Elijah.

"Hey, Babe," Elijah answered on the first ring.

"Did you forget to tell me someone is staying in Condo Omega?" she asked.

"Umm, not that I know of. Why do you ask?"

"I keep hearing bumping, and at one point I thought I heard voices. I heard Rachel leave for the office earlier, so I know it's not her."

"Ok, call security, then, go to my office and lock the door. I'm pulling into the garage right now."

Karyn hated this feeling of fear. She was glad Jaleel was in school during the day. If this was a break-in of some type, she didn't want her nephew traumatized any further. Last year, they had been kidnapped and held against their will.

She did as she was told and slowly made her way to the office and waited. At 38 weeks pregnant, she couldn't do anything fast.

About fifteen minutes later, Karyn heard Elijah calling for her. She opened the door and walked into his arms. "Was there someone over there?" she asked.

Elijah laughed a little, "Yes. I would like for you to meet Gabriella and her daughters, Tiffany and Tierra."

Karyn noticed the beautiful woman and her two girls standing off to the side of the living room. The girls appeared to be about three & ten years old. Karyn put on her best smile and welcomed the woman into her home. She turned back to Elijah wearing her, "I'm confused," look.

"Gabriella, have a seat. I'll get you and the girls something to drink. I need to talk to my wife for a minute." He grabbed Karyn's hand and walked her into the kitchen.

"Okay. Talk," Karyn demanded.

"Yeah, so, this stays between the two of us. No one else knows," Elijah whispered behind the opened refrigerator door.

"Okay. What is it? Who is she?" Karyn asked, confused.

"That's Nehemiah's wife and daughters," he revealed.

"WHAT?" Karyn shouted.

Nehemiah was just arriving into the Fort Lauderdale airport when he got the call from Elijah. He had plans of relaxing in Miami for a few days with his siblings before heading to Gabriella in Indianapolis. He hadn't seen his brothers in over 9 months and needed some time with them after his last mission. His team had discovered three brothers murdered by rebel forces in a Columbian village. The brothers were found still embracing one another.

Upon finding them, he immediately thought of his own brothers. They weren't as close as they used to be, and he was to blame. He didn't keep in communication with them like he should. The love was always there, but they should be closer, and he had planned to remedy that when he returned.

Now, Gabriella was his priority, she had flown from Indianapolis to Miami looking for him. That could only mean, she felt their lives were in danger. Fear would have been the only thing to send her fleeing the place she called home for the last few years.

Her security had been lessened since there was no credible threat against her, and it appeared that Montoya, nor Ortiz, were looking for her. She continued with her regularly check-ins with Jake, but she was allowed to come and go as she wanted, within her neighborhood. She had met friends in her apartment building and had enrolled the girls in a nearby school.

All kinds of crazy thoughts were going through Nehemiah's mind as he raced through the Florida streets to get to her. What if Montoya had found them? Or worse, what if Ortiz found them. There was no credible intelligence that suggested this. Nehemiah tried to shake the thoughts from his head. The only thing that mattered was, she made it safely.

As soon as he entered Elijah's condo, his daughters came running to him.

"Daddy! Daddy!"

"Hey, girls! How are you?" he asked his daughters, enveloping them in a huge hug, but never taking his eyes from Gabriella.

Tiffany started talking first, "Daddy, Mommy said we had to come see you."

"I see." He kissed them both on the cheeks. "Let me talk to Mommy for a minute, okay?

"Okay!" Both girls ran back to the family room where they had been watching cartoons on Uncle Elijah's 80-inch screen television.

He walked toward her and wrapped his arms around her. Her warmth calmed his racing heart. "Gabriella, when did you get here, and why didn't you call me?"

"We arrived yesterday. And, I couldn't call you. I had to throw the phone away." Nehemiah had instructed her that if she ever felt like her life was in danger, toss her cell phone, and immediately travel to his home in Miami. Her name was on the visitor's list, and she had a key and code for the building and Condo Omega.

"Why? What's going on? What happened?" he questioned.

Gabriella looked around and saw Elijah and Karyn staring at them. Karyn was wide-eyed because she had never seen this softer side of Nehemiah.

"It's okay. You know Elijah is okay. Karyn may be pregnant, but she's a fighter. And, my brother and I would never let any harm come to her or you and the girls."

Seeming to accept his response, Gabriella continued. "Last week, I got a call from a blocked number. I didn't answer like you told me. Then, on Monday, a call came from Virginia. I thought it was Jake, but it wasn't. The guy said I know where you are and I'm coming to get you. It sounded like... like..."

"It's okay, Baby. I'm here now." He held her tighter then asked, "Was it, Carlos?"

"Yes, he found us," she sobbed.

Nehemiah and Elijah retreated to Elijah's office, leaving Gabriella and the girls with Karyn in the family room. They were talking girl stuff; mostly about pregnancy, labor, and delivery things. Nehemiah needed to get his mind straight, in order to figure out his next steps. He had to protect his family at all costs.

"Listen, Elijah, she can't stay here. I won't put your family or Moses & Neiko or Rachel in this type of jeopardy."

"Wherever you send her, you need to be able to keep a clear head by knowing she is as safe as possible."

"I agree." Nehemiah lowered his head into his hands. This was not how he had planned his few days off.

"Good. Then, you should agree to send her to the parental units."

"Hell no!" Nehemiah jumped up. "Are you crazy?" he asked, not expecting an answer. "Mom would kill me, then she would kill you for not saying anything."

"What is worse? Mom raising her voice at you, or losing your family? You know being in that fortress with Mom and Dad is way better than anywhere else."

Sending his family to his parents had to be the last resort. His mother would be furious at him for keeping secrets, especially the secret of a whole family. He had to think of another option. At the moment, nothing better was coming to him.

"I'm calling Jake and getting him over here right now," Nehemiah stated, reaching for his cell phone.

There was a scream from the other room. Both men raced into the family room not knowing what to expect. Karyn was on her knees holding her stomach. Gabriella was bent over rubbing her back and coaxing her to take deep breaths through the contractions.

"Karyn, are you okay?" Elijah asked.

"Do I look like I'm okay? I'm in labor," Karyn snapped.

"She had been having light contractions, and then her water broke. I was coming to get you when she screamed," Gabriella told the guys.

"Stop with the yapping and help me up." Karyn looked at Nehemiah and then, at Elijah. "Well, does someone want to get my bag from the room and start moving toward the door? Sheesh, you look like you've never seen a woman in labor before."

Nehemiah helped Karyn to her feet while Elijah jumped into action, racing around the room trying not to forget anything. Gabriella and Nehemiah helped Karyn to the foyer and called for the elevator.

"Are you sure we don't need to call an ambulance?" Elijah asked Gabriella.

"Trust me, this is her first birth, she will be a long time. Her contractions are barely ten minutes apart."

Elijah was a nervous wreck like most new fathers, but he was hiding his fear well. He had been through this a few times with his sisters. His siblings had a combined fifteen children, and he was on hand for six of those births. No one was around when Ruth went into labor and Elijah almost had to deliver his nephew, Rusty.

The elevator doors opened with one of the guards waiting for them. The guard would override the elevator system and take them straight to the parking garage without stopping. Elijah promised to call as soon as he could to update them.

After making sure his brother and sister-in-law were okay and off to the hospital, Nehemiah took his family back to his condo. His last mission had lasted three months. He had missed his family so much that his judgment was clouded during the mission, and he almost botched the entire assignment.

Now, he had his wife snuggled next to him on his left, and his girls asleep on his right. This was the life he had wanted since before Tierra was born. Her birth brought final clarity to his life. He knew exactly what he wanted. His retirement paperwork had finally been accepted, and it should be approved within the next sixty days.

"Nehemiah, how long are you home for?" Gabriella asked.

"Two weeks. I was hoping to come see you in Indy when Elijah called me."

"I'm sorry to be so much trouble." She bit on her lip like she would do when she didn't know what to say.

"You are no trouble to me. I love you and my beautiful daughters." He was being honest; he knew of no greater love.

Nehemiah pulled her in closer. Thinking about what Elijah told him, taking his family to his parents may be the only answer. His parents lived on a few acres of land in Suffolk, VA, just outside of Virginia Beach. They had a state-of-the-art security system installed when Elijah became "Evolution," and the fans and paparazzi became relentless. Both of his parents were trained in firearms. His father was a retired Navy Master Chief and a master shooter. His mother, never wanting to be left out, was also trained in firearms. There were no other good options in this situation.

He took his sleeping daughters to bed before returning to the living room to talk with Gabriella. He had to tell her the plan and ask those questions he never wanted to ask her years ago. When she gave her statement and testimony to the government, he promised himself he would not ask questions, and he would not read the report.

Rejoining her on the sofa with a glass of wine for her and a beer for himself, he had to ask. "Gabriella, it's time we have a crucial conversation. I was hoping to get Ortiz off the streets and hopefully catch Carlos up in the middle. It looks like they are bringing the fight to me." Nehemiah looked deeply into her eyes. Five years had been a long time, and he, nor, the government had ever gotten any closer to shutting down the trafficking in Puerto Rico.

"I need you to tell me everything you know about Carlos' business, and Ortiz," he said.

Gabriella jumped from the sofa and began pacing. Nehemiah could see the fear in her eyes.

"Why? Why have you never asked me before?" she asked. "I told the agents everything I know."

He held his head in his hands and dropped them between his knees. He never wanted to believe the truth about her. He knew she was involved in the trafficking somehow, but he didn't want to hear her confirm her involvement.

She walked away from him and toward the patio doors. She wouldn't look at him. Nehemiah stood and walked toward her. He wrapped his arms around her waist to give her support and comfort. "No matter what you say, I love you; and I will always be here for you."

There was silence for a few minutes before Gabriella began to speak. "I was 19 when I met Carlos. We met on the track team at the University of the Virgin Islands. He was smooth, said all the right things, but after that year, he didn't return."

Nehemiah felt her shiver, and he wrapped his arms tightly around her. They gazed out into the Miami skyline. He didn't rush her to speak. Finally, she started again.

"When I returned home, my first job was at the Ocean Breeze resort in the human resources department. I ran into Carlos in the hotel. He remembered me and took me to dinner. He wined and dined me, and I fell deeper and deeper in love with him. When I got pregnant with Tiffany, that's when he became abusive." Nehemiah felt her hot tears fall on his arms. He suddenly whisked her off her feet and into his arms and moved them back to the sofa. He cradled her in his arms and encouraged her to continue.

"His abuse was verbal, at first. He became physical after Tiffany was born. He only wanted me for a showpiece around his friends. While I was pregnant, he couldn't show me off anymore. Then, he became jealous of Tiffany. He'd get upset whenever I tried to take care of her, feed her, bathe her. He would just get mad." She began crying again but held it together to continue. "Then, he forced me to take a position as the head of housekeeping. I had to leave my office job for a service position. Within a month, he had me stealing items from guest rooms. He would make threats to hurt Tiffany to get to me."

Gabriella had to stop talking, again. The pain was evident in her voice as she tried to speak through sobs, but her strength kept her talking. "Six months before you met me, he used me to recruit new young housekeepers. Young girls from the smaller villages. After a few weeks, they would come up missing. I knew he was selling them to his rich friends, but I never had any proof. Until the day I came to you. I gave you Tiffany for safe-keeping. I went back to the house where we lived and grabbed his external drives from his safe."

Nehemiah flinched like he had been sucker punched. She had physical evidence against Carlos and had never said a word. Why would she hold on to those items? He wanted to ask her, to blame her, but he couldn't. He knew how hard it was for her to leave her home and everything she knew to move to Indiana.

"Where are the drives now?" he asked her.

"I transferred the files to my Faith bracelet and put his drives back. My bracelet is also a drive." She lifted her wrist and showed him the rubber bracelet that separated and had a USB drive on the end.

He knew the bracelet very well. It was the only jewelry she wore when they left San Juan. She always had it on, and she only removed it to take showers or wash dishes. Even then, she would place it in her pocket or on the bathroom sink.

Nehemiah held her for several more minutes before taking her to bed. There, he held her some more. He could see the fear in her eyes. It was a look he never wanted to see from her. He had to do whatever it took for her to never look that way again.

"We have a friendly to your 9 o'clock."

"Where? I don't see anyone?" Angel whispered. Then, he heard her voice.

"Do you have my money?" she asked the leader of the group.

Angel was confused; what was she doing there? How did she get into the ballroom with the hostages? One of the gunmen walked over to the leader and uttered something to him. The leader took a step back and held his gun up to her head.

"You thought you could trick me. Stupid American." *He pulled the trigger.*

Nehemiah sprang from the bed in a cold sweat. He looked over to see if he had awakened Gabriella. She was still sound asleep. Not wanting to wake her, he tip-toed from the room and moved down the hall to the guest bathroom.

He needed a hot shower. Not that he thought that would erase his nightmares, but it usually made him feel better. Somehow, he needed to find out why he was continuing to relive that moment over and over again. The counseling didn't help, and now the nightmares were coming more frequently.

The next morning, Nehemiah was preparing breakfast for his girls. They loved when he made pecan honey pancakes with the special maple syrup. His face would beam with love and pride whenever he thought of his daughters and wife. They were the best part of him, and he hated he couldn't share their love with the world like the rest of his family.

He hadn't slept much through the night, working on details for his next move. Going to his parents seemed inevitable. The Boldens were a tight-knit family, and they stuck together no matter what. His siblings would want to help in any way, but with them having families, it made it hard for Nehemiah to lean on them. Elijah knowing the details of what was happening was one thing but getting a very pregnant Neiko and Moses involved would be something else altogether. He had to find a way that didn't involve them.

There was a hard knock at his front door. Nehemiah rushed to answer before the knocking woke his family. He grabbed his firearm from the hall table's secure drawer – he was being extra cautious. The man standing on the other side of the door was not familiar to Nehemiah. Immediately on guard, he opened the door slightly.

"Yeah?"

"Hey, umm is Elijah or Karyn here?" the man asked.

"Who wants to know?"

"Oh, yeah, I'm sorry. I'm Scott. Scott Heller. Monica Diaz is my sister. I'm in town to relax, and Moses and Neiko said I can crash at their place while they are in Atlanta."

Monica was the best friend of his sisters-in-law, Karyn and Neiko. He remembered Moses mentioning that she had a brother who was in the Navy and stationed in Guam.

"Okay, sorry about that, Scott." He returned the firearm to the drawer and fully opened the door. "I'm Nehemiah. Nice to meet you."

"Nehemiah, right, the secret brother. Military, right?" Scott reached out to shake his hand.

"Yeah Navy, like you. Monica and Neiko told me about you. On leave?"

"Nah, retired. Twenty years was enough for me. What about you?"

"I hear you. Retirement paperwork on its way up the chain of command as we speak."

"Alright. Well, Elijah was supposed to have the keys for me and they're not answering at their place."

"Oh right…Karyn went into labor last night. Come on in. Let me grab my cell phone and see if I have any missed texts or calls. I had my own issues last night or I would be at the hospital with them."

Nehemiah found his phone in the living room, and sure enough, he had 4 missed calls and 7 text messages. "Yep, looks like we have two new baby Boldens. Elijah Jr. and Erica Rene were born at five this morning. Mom and babies are doing good."

"That's great news," Scott replied.

"You want to stay for breakfast?" Nehemiah asked, not wanting to be rude to a fellow shipmate.

"Thanks for asking. Don't mind if I do."

The two men easily grew more comfortable with one another while they talked about the military and the transition back into civilian life. Nehemiah was finishing up with breakfast when both his daughters came running into the kitchen.

"Daddy! Daddy! You're still here!" Tiffany exclaimed, jumping into his arms.

Nehemiah caught her in midair, smothering her with kisses. She wasn't used to him still being in the house the next morning. He usually left while everyone was sleeping to prevent seeing his girls cry watching him leave.

Tierra waited patiently for her turn to be lifted in the air and smothered in kisses by her father.

"Daddy, who is that?" Tierra asked, staying close to Nehemiah's side when she saw Scott sitting at the breakfast bar.

Nehemiah had temporarily forgotten Scott was still in the kitchen with him.

"Baby Girl, this is Mr. Scott. He is a friend of Uncle Elijah's. Can you say hello to Mr. Scott?"

Tierra shyly whispered, "Hi." Tiffany, not shy at all, said, "Hello Mr. Scott. You eating breakfast with us?"

"If that's okay with you?" Scott replied.

Tierra smiled and answered, "Daddy makes the best pancakes."

Gabriella joined the group soon after the girls and was introduced to Scott. They enjoyed a breakfast of pancakes, eggs, sausage, and fresh fruit. Tiffany held the conversation down for the adults.

"Mr. Scott, do you live here?"

"Ah, no. I don't really live anywhere right now."

"How come?" She innocently asked, while taking a big bite of her pancakes.

"That's enough questions, *Mija*. Eat your food." Gabriella stopped her inquisitive daughter before she said too much.

Children didn't have a filter or know how to keep things to themselves. Gabriella found out the hard way when Tiffany told the clerk at the store that her daddy protects the world.

*****

After breakfast, they sat and talked awhile before Nehemiah gave Scott the key to Moses' and Neiko's condo. Scott thanked him for breakfast and went to settle into his temporary home. He looked around the condo, and his first thoughts were they must be really rich. Then, he remembered, yeah they were really rich.

Rachel was the president and CEO of the family recording studio, record label, and production company, while Moses was the Chief Operating/Financial Officer. Neiko worked as the V.P. of Marketing for Scott's brother-in-law, Ric Diaz. Scott couldn't really comprehend the wealth since he was a military man. Working for Uncle Sam didn't afford him the type of luxuries he saw in this condo.

In the corner of the great room was a beautiful Fazioli Brunei concert grand piano. He only knew that from overhearing the conversation Moses was having with some other guys at Neiko and Karyn's baby shower a few weeks ago. Apparently, the piano was one of a kind.

Everything in the condo appeared extravagant and very clean. There wasn't any dust to be found in the room. The kitchen was also immaculate. He started feeling uneasy being in there. He was afraid he might accidentally break something worth more than his net worth. It was like walking around a museum or someplace fancy when your mother would threaten you not to touch anything.

Scott was admiring a few crystal vases on the mantel over the fireplace when the youngest Bolden sister, Rachel, bounced down the stairs, wearing headphones and humming along to the music. He stood still and just watched her for a few seconds. She was petite and looked amazingly younger than her 29 years. He had first met her at the baby shower.

She was breathtakingly beautiful, wearing a pair of ripped jeans and a t-shirt that said, "Keep Calm and Worship." Scott took a deep breath and moved away from the mantel toward her. Rachel must have caught the movement from the corner of her eye, because she screamed and jumped.

"I didn't mean to startle you," Scott apologized.

Taking the headphones from her ears, "Geesh, Scott. You shouldn't sneak up on people like that."

He laughed. "I didn't think I was sneaking up on you since I was in the room first and I didn't know you were here. By the way, don't you live next door?"

"I do live next door. I was making sure everything upstairs was clean for your stay. The guest bedroom had been set-up as Moses' art studio…. a real hot mess."

"I see," Scott responded. There was an awkward silence, and he waited for her to say more. When she didn't say anything or appear to leave, Scott asked, "Rachel, where can I get some really greasy food around here?"

"Greasy?"

"Yeah, like a Coney dog or chili cheese fries. I'm missing home."

Scott had spent the last few weeks processing out of the military from the naval base in Jacksonville. Instead of going home to Detroit, he decided to check out Miami first.

"I know a spot. Just like Lafayette Coney Island."

"What do you know about Lafayette?" he asked.

"Let's just say, I spent some time there." She smiled, and Scott's heart melted. "I'll take you to my spot. Let me change my clothes and I…"

"What's wrong with what you are wearing? It's not a fancy dinner. It's just hotdogs and fries." In his opinion, all she needed was a pair of shoes, and they could leave.

"Scott, you will have to learn. It's Miami. I'm somewhat of a celebrity around here, and I could be photographed at any time. I must look my best. Meet me in the lobby in 20 minutes."

In a flash, she was up the stairs and out the patio doors. Scott wondered why she would go that way to get ready, but then he remembered the four condos shared a rooftop swimming pool. He didn't think he would ever get accustomed to the lifestyles of the rich and famous. The only seemingly ordinary person in the Bolden family was Nehemiah. Scott chucked that up to the fact he was a military man.

True to her word, Rachel was in the lobby in 20 minutes. She kept her jeans on, but changed out her t-shirt for a blue, flowing blouse and a pair of dark sunglasses. She wore a pair of simple blue stilettos.

He was also impressed that she was on-time. In his experience, women tended to want to be fashionably late, which annoyed him. Being intentionally late was just disrespectful to the time of the person waiting. In his book, Rachel just gained a few cool points.

Scott was surprised that Rachel took him to a hole in the wall spot, that was walking distance from the condos. He was sure she would fall or stumble in those shoes, but she seemed very comfortable walking in heels.

The booths in the restaurant had leather seats covered in silver electrical tape, and it was a little smoky, which the hostess explained was aroma.

"So, how did you find this place?" he asked Rachel after being seated in one of the booths in the back.

"What do you mean?" Rachel looked up from her menu.

"I mean, it's not somewhere I would think you would frequent."

"Why? Because you think I am too bourgeois for a place like this."

He cringed with the knowledge that he was messing up where she was concerned. Scott choked on the proverbial foot in his mouth. He was saved from responding when the waitress approached their table.

"Honey, you want your usual?" she asked Rachel.

"Yes! And, add some extra jalapenos," Rachel responded, excitedly.

"What about you, cutie?" The waitress turned her attention to Scott.

Scott blushed. He wasn't used to women using that term so loosely. The waitress had to be over 60 years of age. He figured she wasn't flirting with him, and that was the way she greeted everyone, but after taking his order, the waitress gave a wink of the eye before walking away.

"Someone has an admirer," Rachel teased him.

"I think she is older than my mother."

"Well, you know what they say? Age ain't nothing but a number, throwing down ain't nothing but a thang," she sang the lyrics from the Aaliyah classic.

"A-ha! So, the music mogul does sing."

Rachel shrugged and ignored his statement.

Chapter 3

The temperature was a moderate 70 degrees; and Nehemiah had no idea why he was sweating so profusely. He believed it had everything to do with having to tell his parents what was going on, and about his family. Jaclyn Bolden was a formidable and loving woman. She was the best mother to seven children, and a great wife to a career Navy man. His father was less scary than his mother. She was who he was most afraid of.

She would never understand the decision he had to make, keeping his family a secret. The first reaction was not the one Nehemiah feared, it was the reaction she would have after she had time to process everything. Jaclyn Bolden was a kind woman to everyone she met, but she held her children to higher expectations.

Nehemiah tried to prepare Gabriella for his parents. He didn't think he had done a good job, because she was still shaking when they crossed the Virginia state line. She was staying quiet, and that was another indicator that she, too, was terrified. Usually, she talked with him about everything.

He slowly pulled up to the gate leading to his parents' estate. After entering the code on the key pad, the gate slowly lifted, allowing him access. Nehemiah felt the driveway was the equivalent of walking the plank. Lots of questions he couldn't answer lie beyond the trees.

Nehemiah parked next to a black Mercedes Benz; it was a gift from Elijah to his parents. The license plate read BOLD1, which meant, it was his mom's car and she was home. The moment of truth had finally arrived. He closed his eyes and squeezed really tight, hoping this was all a dream.

Unfortunately, when he opened his eyes, he realized this wasn't a dream, and he was facing the music. Nehemiah turned to his wife and said, "Time to meet my family."

Dr. Jaclyn Bolden stood on the front porch and waited for Nehemiah to exit the vehicle. She was a remarkable and accomplished woman. Being a tenured professor of Religious Studies at Old Dominion University, some people thought her to be a superwoman. She had obtained five university degrees while raising seven children and traveling with her military husband to every duty station. Her education included bachelor's degrees in communication and international marketing, a master's degree in business administration with a concentration in organizational leadership, a master's degree in world religion, and a doctorate degree in divinity. She was a force to be reckoned with.

The girls had fallen asleep in the back seat of the car. Gabriella got out of the car first and reached in the back for Tierra. Nehemiah did the same on his side and grabbed Tiffany. With measured steps, they slowly approached the house under the watchful eye of Jaclyn Bolden.

"Hi, Mom." Nehemiah didn't know what else to say as he watched the different expressions cross his mother's face. She appeared happy to see him, but also cautious.

"Well, who do we have here?" Jaclyn's demeanor had shifted to care and concern when she saw the girls asleep in their arms.

"Mom, this is Gabriella and our daughters, Tiffany and Tierra," he said, holding his breath and waiting for the first shoe to drop. Shockingly, it didn't come.

"Well, come in. Put those girls down in the guest room. It must have been an exhausting drive from Miami." She, then, cut her eyes at Nehemiah. There goes the fire he was expecting.

Someone must have told her they were coming. She didn't have the reaction he thought she would have. It had to be Karyn; only she would betray him like this and spill the beans before he got there. His sister-in-law was sweet and loving but couldn't stand keeping secrets. Too many secrets had been kept in her life.

He and Gabriella placed both girls in the king-sized bed, removing only their jackets and shoes. Before returning to the great room where he knew his mother was awaiting their return, he grabbed Gabriella by the shoulders and gazed into her eyes. They silently communicated with one another. Everything would be alright.

Jaclyn had placed a pitcher of sweet tea and a tray of cheese and crackers on the table when Nehemiah walked in holding Gabriella's hand. They took a seat on the sofa and waited. The quietness in the room was eerie; no one said anything, no music in the background, nothing.

Jaclyn finally broke the silence. "You can begin whenever you are ready. You should know the initial questions I have. And, don't stop talking until I say so." She reached for her glass of tea, leaned back in her seat to get comfortable, and waited.

"Mother, I didn't want you to find out like this. Keeping her hidden away was for her security." Jaclyn didn't appear satisfied, so Nehemiah continued. "Her life is still in danger. Coming here was our final option."

His mother placed her glass on the table and stood, wiping her hands down the front of her dress. She looked back and forth between Nehemiah and Gabriella. Her expression was unreadable and making Nehemiah tense. She just stood over them, looking.

"Mother, please? Say something," Nehemiah begged in a hushed whisper.

"Well, Nehemiah, I'm not sure what you want me to say. For years, I knew you were keeping secrets. I know your job requires a level of discretion, but this is not something you keep from your family," Jaclyn stated, without raising her voice. "Gabriella, my anger is not directed at you. You are innocent in the deception of my son."

"Deception? Mom I couldn't say anything," Nehemiah shouted.

"Don't raise your voice to your mother," Jeremiah Bolden entered the room. His presence commanded attention. The patriarch of the Bolden family and a 35-year Navy Veteran Master Chief Petty Officer, was used to respect from his sailors and his family. "What seems to be the problem?"

Jaclyn rolled her shoulder back, lifted her head, and visibly relaxed. "Gabriella, this is my husband, Jeremiah. Jeremiah, your daughter-in-law."

Here it comes, Nehemiah thought. Gabriella had remained silent and was now trembling next to him. He tried to comfort her by rubbing his hand across her back. *"Todo estará bien,"* Nehemiah whispered to Gabriella.

She didn't stop shivering, nor would she look up. Jeremiah noticed Gabriella's nervousness and had not wanted to scare her any further than she already was.

"Bienvenido a la familia, Gabriella," Jeremiah welcomed her to the family and held his arms out indicating he wanted a hug from his new daughter-in-law.

Before she stood, Gabriella looked back to Nehemiah for reassurance. He nodded, giving her the strength she needed to stand and return the gesture. He knew his father would be the peacekeeper at the moment.

Nehemiah understood why his mother was upset. She had every right to be angry at him for not telling her. The truth was, he was afraid of what his mother would think after the years of partying and having different girls around. He was worried his mother would think of this relationship as a fleeting moment like the rest, but this was different. There were children involved.

Gabriella had been the first woman he wanted to share his life with. She was his equal in so many ways. The others had been women for the moment, and he never led any of them to believe otherwise. Even his relationship with Chrystal was meant to be temporary.

"Oh, but there is more," Jaclyn added. "I'm going to fix us more tea and lunch; we may be here for a while." She strode off to the kitchen in a dignified huff.

Nehemiah knew it wasn't going to be easy coming home and bringing his family. He let Elijah talk him into this. Now that he was here, there was no going back.

"So, what's the other news," Jeremiah took a seat across from the couple. He then looked to Gabriella and asked, "Are you pregnant?"

"Oh, no sir," she quickly answered.

Nehemiah noticed disappointment in his father's eyes. The man had over fifteen grandchildren, not including Tierra and Tiffany. Didn't he think that was enough? Probably not for a man who was the youngest of twelve children and had seven children of his own. Jeremiah believed the myth, "the more the merrier."

"Dad, she's not pregnant; but we do have two girls. Tiffany and Tierra. They are asleep in the guest room."

The news of two more grandchildren returned the light to Jeremiah's eyes. You could almost see the pride in his face, and he hadn't even met them yet. Nehemiah was starting to feel better about his decision to come home. Nobody protected family like family.

On the way to his parents' house, Nehemiah had called his siblings to ensure they would be available for an emergency family conference call. He needed everyone to know what was going on and what needed to be done. Naomi and her family lived nearby in Chesapeake, and they were due to arrive at any minute. Ruth and her family split their time living between Virginia and North Carolina, where her husband was from. Since she home-schooled her children, it made the back and forth easy. At the current time,

Ruth was in North Carolina and would be joining by call just like Moses, Elijah, Aaron, and Rachel.

"Dad, I think we need to move to your office. I have contacted the family for a conference call to discuss everything that is going on with Gabriella and me."

Jeremiah nodded, understanding what Nehemiah was not saying. They had a way of communicating with one another with just a few looks. Nehemiah had given his father the all-important, life or death, look; and his father understood the seriousness of the current situation.

Arriving right on time, Naomi, her husband Greg, and her rambunctious bunch of kids came through the front door. As soon as the children saw Uncle Miah, they ran full speed and toppled him over.

"Uncle Miah, when did you get here?"

"Uncle Miah, did you bring us anything?"

"Uncle Miah, who's that lady?"

The kids fired off questions; and Nehemiah quickly realized it wasn't just the adults he had to talk to. The children of the family would have more questions, too. Once they found out they had more cousins, the games would begin. Unable to prove anything, the adults in the family were sure that the children had some type of underground communication network. They would pass information around to one another from state to state, and no one knew how they did it. Nehemiah also thought they had their own language. He had caught Aaron's sons, Marcus and Malachi, speaking in code once. Of course, they denied everything.

"Hey! Y'all, get off your uncle. Go to the backyard and play. We are about to talk about grown folk's business," Naomi told her children.

After he was able to get up from the floor, he saw his daughters standing in the hallway. Gabriella must have seen them, too, because she swiftly headed toward them.

"Gabriella, bring them in here," Nehemiah instructed.

When they saw their father, they, too, jumped on him, but didn't hold him down. "Hey, little munchkins," he said to his nieces and nephews. "These are your cousins, Tiffany and Tierra. Girls, can you say 'hi?'"

All six of the children were somewhat apprehensive about the two new additional cousins. They all squeaked out a soft "hi," but unsure of what to do or say next.

"Hey guys," Naomi said to her children. "Why don't you take Tiffany and Tierra outside and show them the playground Grampy built for you?"

The children got excited, except for Tierra. She was holding on to her father for dear life. Tiffany held out her hand to her sister and told her it would be okay.

"It's okay, Tiffany. You go play. I will keep Tierra," Gabriella told her.

"Ok!" Tiffany replied. And, just like that, the whirlwind of small humans went out the back door, all laughter and smiles.

Jaclyn re-entered the front foyer where everyone was standing. "Did I hear my babies?" She walked over to her daughter and son-in-law, greeting them with a hug and kiss.

"Hey, Mom. The kids took Tiffany to the playground out back," Naomi told her.

Nehemiah noticed a change in his mother's demeanor from earlier. Either, she was happy to see Naomi and Greg, or she was genuinely accepting the drama that was unfolding in her home. He just hoped she continued to accept what was coming next.

"Mom, we are going to meet in Dad's office. I need the whole family to hear what's going on," Nehemiah said.

Jaclyn looked around the room, to each person, beaming with pride. Even as she looked to Nehemiah and Gabriella, she smiled even bigger. That act of kindness caused Gabriella to relax more.

The family moved into the office where Jeremiah was connecting the family by video conferencing and Jaclyn was placing lunch on the desk. She had prepared vegetables with dip, a fruit tray, and chicken salad.

Nehemiah may not always show it, but he was eternally grateful for his family. With the secret of his family out, he thought it was time to start appreciating his siblings and parents more. He would come around more often, interact with his nieces and nephews, help to form bonds with his girls. It was long past due.

The computer screen started chiming as each of his siblings' faces popped on the screen. First, Elijah and Karyn joined from the hospital, then, Ruth, along with her husband, Carson. Moses and Neiko were in Atlanta and joined from the Diaz Inc. offices. Because the family was so close to the Diaz family, Ric and Monica were included in the meeting. Aaron and Danielle met at the Diaz building and joined the meeting with them. Last to log-in was Rachel, always wanting to make a grand appearance.

"Hey, family! Sorry I'm late. I just got back from a late lunch," Rachel explained.

A voice could be heard from the background saying, "See ya later." Rachel briefly looked away from the camera and smiled.

"Who is there with you?" Moses asked, in his big brother voice.

"Oh, that was Scott...Monica's brother." Rachel saw Monica on one of the many boxes on her screen and started waving.

Nehemiah thought maybe Scott should also be in attendance. He was a military guy trained in security and surveillance. His skills may come in handy.

"Hey Rachel, call him back over. He should hear this, too," Nehemiah said.

After about forty-five minutes of explaining the situation to the family and answering questions, Nehemiah had an all-in assurance from every family member.

The current plan was for Gabriella and the girls to stay with the elder Boldens. Nehemiah and Jake would ensure the security system his parents had was updated and fully functional. Two security details would be assigned to the estate in the evenings. His dad could handle things during the day. Nehemiah assured everyone that no one else was in any type of danger.

"So, Miah," Moses spoke up to ask the question no one really wanted an answer to. "What are you going to do?"

Nehemiah didn't even blink when he said, "I'm going to find and neutralize the threat to my family."

*****

Jaclyn didn't feel comfortable with the words Nehemiah chose to use. Sure, he was protective of his family, but neutralize also meant kill, and that was something she was opposed to him doing, outside of his line of work. She knew Nehemiah was involved with some special forces type of stuff, but she didn't need, nor, want to hear him talk about it.

After the family conference call ended, the men decided to check out some new project Jeremiah was working on in the garage. Naomi and Gabriella retreated to the family room. As the family was leaving, Jaclyn grabbed ahold of her son and practically dragged him into an empty guest room. She could see he was preparing himself for her lecture. Instead of a lecture, she embraced her son tightly. For several minutes, Jaclyn just held Nehemiah. She needed him to know that while she may be angry, she still loved him.

She stepped back, but continued to hold his arms, "You didn't have to keep her a secret. You robbed of us of a relationship with her and the girls. How long have you been **married**?"

Nehemiah sat on the edge of the bed and waited for his mother to follow. He looked down at his feet, first, before looking at her. She knew that tortured look. She had seen it many times in her son. He was holding something back; a pain that he couldn't let go of.

"Mom," he struggled to say that little bit. "I didn't plan for this to happen. I didn't even want to fall in love with her, but I did." He dropped his head, again.

Jaclyn grabbed his chin to force his head up. She stared into his eyes as if trying to read his soul. Whenever she did this to her boys, their hard-core exterior faded away. They knew she meant business and were no longer able to be tough.

"How. Long. Have. You. Been. Married?" she enunciated each word while staring into his eyes.

"Two years," he answered.

"Tiffany is at least 10 years-old. Is she yours?"

"No, ma'am, but Tierra is mine."

"Oh, boy. Anyone can look at Tierra and know she is your child, but Tiffany looks just like her mother. It doesn't matter. They are both beautiful, and they are both my granddaughters," Jaclyn smiled.

She continued, "But let me go on record as saying, I am not thrilled with the way in which you have handled this. I can see you are also dealing with some other kind of hurt. It's consuming you from the inside. This hurt you are dealing with, you need to talk with someone."

"Mom! I'm not going to a shrink or a doctor. I can handle it."

"Nehemiah, you have been self-medicating this pain of yours for years."

"What are you talking about? I don't take drugs; not even pain relievers or cold medicine."

"I'm not talking about drugs, I'm talking about your healing. You can't heal from this pain by yourself. If you won't go to a counselor or talk to your parents, then get on your knees and talk to God."

"God can't fix me," he whispered.

"You know that's not the truth. You turned your face away from me when you said it. That tells me you are ashamed for even thinking it." Jaclyn paused to give him time to think about what he had done. "Nehemiah, you were not named that by accident. God gave that name to me when you were born. Nehemiah, in the bible, was a great man who was able to rebuild a city and restore order to the Jews. He did all of this while fighting the enemy from all sides. This is your legacy. Rebuild what was destroyed in your life…in Gabriella's life. Pray to the Father and ask Him for guidance. Once you keep quiet and listen, He will show you that you are loved and he will show you the way."

She stared at her son; the one she inwardly called the fighter. She knew he would be the one to follow his father into the military and he would be the one to stand up for family and keep them all safe. He was their protector and always had been, Jaclyn had no doubt that whatever demons he was struggling with, he would find his way.

No other words were said between the two. None were needed. Jaclyn kissed his cheek and left him alone to his thoughts. She understood he had to make this decision for himself and for his family.

Chapter 4

Gabriella spent a lot of time talking with Naomi and Jaclyn while the children played in the yard. Her new family was genuinely interested in learning about her and the girls. She was nervous when she first arrived at the Bolden's home, and Jaclyn's initial reaction to meeting her was less than ideal; but after Nehemiah was able to explain the situation to everyone, Gabriella felt the warmth and love of family toward her and her girls.

No one asked too many questions about how she got involved with her ex-husband, and Gabriella found that to be puzzling. One would think most people would want to know more about the stranger they were risking their lives for. Instead, they were all accepting of what Nehemiah had told them. And, they seemed to be very protective; this was something Gabriella wasn't used to.

Gabriella didn't have a family to depend on. That was how she got involved with Carlos in the first place. In the beginning, he felt like family, someone she could lean on and talk to. When her mother died, she was all alone and looking for love anywhere she could find it, but that love turned out to be one-sided, and then, violent.

The Boldens were like an unreal family. Gabriella had only seen families like this on television or in movies. Naomi immediately started treating her like they had known each other for years. She had offered to bring her children to the house every day so the girls would have someone to play with. Ruth and her family were planning a trip to meet and get to know her and the girls. Moses and Neiko were expecting a baby soon and promised to get there as soon as possible to meet her in person.

To say they were overwhelming was an understatement. She never knew people could be this understanding and loving. Nehemiah had tried to prepare her for them. He told her his siblings were going to love her and want to spend time with her. He mentioned that they were a tight group, but she didn't believe they would be this open and forward.

Overnight, she went from a family of four to a family of over twenty. They had known that Nehemiah had a dangerous career, but recently learned that because of his job, he would leave her and the girls alone much of the time. The Boldens promised that would not happen, again. Gabriella would tear up every time she thought about the huge family she now belonged to.

When she and the girls left Indiana, they had only the clothes on their back and whatever she could shove into two duffel bags. The girls had no toys and very little clothing. Naomi and Ruth both offered to take her shopping as soon as possible. Gabriella would soon learn that the Bolden women loved to shop.

"Gabriella, I want you to relax while you're here," Jaclyn told her. "You and my granddaughters are safe. We won't let any harm come to you or them."

"Thank you, Mrs. Bolden. Everyone has been so kind," she held back her tears.

"Stop that. You can call me Mom, Mother, or Jaclyn. That's what family is for." Jaclyn sat beside Gabriella at the breakfast bar in the kitchen. "Honey, I know Nehemiah had his reasons for keeping you and my beautiful grandchildren a secret, but that doesn't change that you are family. You are a Bolden." She grabbed both of Gabriella's hands and smiled. "We stick together, and we protect our own."

"My son has always been in search of something. Never quite finding it, but I can see the love he has for you and the girls. And I can see the love you have for him. I think he may have found what he was looking for."

"What is that?" Gabriella asked, unsure if she wanted to hear the answer or not.

"I think he was in search of a love that he couldn't get from his parents or his siblings, but the love of a good woman. A love that would lift him above his hurt."

"You don't even know me. All of the trouble I am causing. How could you think I am a good woman for Nehemiah?"

"Because, he chose you." Jaclyn patted Gabriella's hand for reassurance. "Now, what would you like for dinner? We don't eat much pork around here, but I have plenty of chicken and fish."

"Thank you. Thank you so very much." Gabriella started crying, again. Jaclyn embraced her in a tight and comforting hug. "I'm sorry for crying so much. I have never had a family like this. Growing up, it was just me and my mom."

"Well, now you have another mother in me, a father, a host of brothers and sisters; plus all these kids. I stopped counting at fifteen," Jaclyn laughed.

Naomi laughed along with her mother. "That's not true. She knows how many grands she has. Seriously, Gabriella, we don't have to know anything other than that Nehemiah loves you, and that's enough for us. We love you, too."

"I guess I can't get over the why or the how. How could you love someone you just met?" Gabriella asked.

"Well, let me tell you all about God's love." Jaclyn held Gabriella's hands and walked over to the sofa in the family room. Naomi followed behind them and joined them on the sofa. "We can love others because He first loved us. I raised my family to love others as Christ loved us. In the Bible, First John, chapter four, verse seven, it says, *'Dear Friends, let us love one another, for love comes from God.'* I don't need to know anything about you to love you. Because, I love God and God is Love."

"Do you believe in God?" Naomi asked, full of concern.

"Yes, I do. My mother was Catholic, but not devout. Since marrying Nehemiah, he makes sure to pray with us every time he calls or visits."

"He prays with you or for you?" Jaclyn asked.

Gabriella was confused by the question. She didn't realize there was a difference. Prayer was prayer in her mind, but as she thought back on the prayers that he recited with the girls and the prayers he recited with her, she would have to say he prayed for her and not for himself.

"I guess he prays for me. He never includes himself in the prayers. Always for our safety."

"That's what I thought," Jaclyn murmured under her breath. "You have a family now. Probably more family than any one person needs, but we are full of love. And, we pray for one another and ourselves."

Nehemiah, his father, and brother-in-law started the grill for dinner. They children had burgers and grilled veggies, while the adults had grilled chicken. The evening felt like a planned family gathering, and there was no more talk of anyone being in danger. There was just fun being had by everyone.

Gabriella kept going back to the conversation she had with Jaclyn about God's love. After bathing the girls and putting them in bed, Gabriella sunk into the whirlpool tub and tried to relax. Everything was happening so fast; and beneath her tough exterior, she was scared to death.

She had no delusions about her past, and she knew she wouldn't be able to live in secrecy forever, but Gabriella had hoped that Nehemiah or the government would have solved this issue by now. Instead, they were no closer to finding her ex-husband, and no sign of Ortiz. She leaned her head back and prayed, then cried. Her cries weren't quiet; they were loud sobs of anguish.

Nehemiah entered the room and didn't immediately see Gabriella. Then, he heard her in the bathroom. When he walked in, she had her eyes closed and was bawling. "Hey, baby, please don't cry," he said, kneeling beside the tub. He reached in and gently pulled her out. He grabbed the oversized towel from the rack and wrapped her body in the plush softness. They sat on the floor of the bathroom, and Nehemiah let her cry.

Gabriella cried herself to sleep in his arms. He gently placed her in the bed, covered her with the duvet and quietly left the room. She awakened early in the morning to an empty bed. Nehemiah was gone. This is how it always was with them. She never wanted to see him leave, and he hated to leave them.

*****

Nehemiah was six hours into his drive back to Miami when Jake called him. "What's up, Jake?"

"Where are you right now?"

"Cruising down Interstate 95. I just passed Savannah. What's the problem?"

"I'm going to meet you in Jacksonville at the NCIS office. There is information we need to move on right now," Jake ended the call.

Nehemiah would be in Jacksonville within two hours. He hoped whatever was going on had something to do with finding Ortiz and Carlos. Nothing else mattered. He had to keep his family safe.

Three hours later, Nehemiah sat in a closed door, sound proof meeting room with Jake, Master Chief McEntire, and Captain Jones of NCIS.

"Nothing said here is to go beyond this room," Captain Jones instructed. He tossed three top-secret envelopes on the table. Each man grabbing one and opening its contents.

"We have found Manuel Ortiz. He has been lying low in Belize. His right-hand man, Carlos Montoya has been running operations in San Juan."

"Well, let's go get him!" Nehemiah was ready to end this threat to his family. It was past time that Ortiz and Montoya were taken care of.

"There's more. We have evidence that Gabriella Montoya has been in communication with her ex-husband."

Nehemiah felt a sinking feeling in his stomach and a tightening in his throat. She told him that Carlos had called her. There was no way Gabriella had been the one to contact Carlos. She had fled her comfort zone in Indianapolis, risked her life and the lives of their children to get to the safe place in Miami. She was afraid, and Nehemiah would know if she was faking that kind of fear.

"Stop! Stop!" Nehemiah yelled. "There is no way Gabriella Bolden has been in contact with her ex-husband."

"Bolden, look at the information in the folder." Nehemiah opened the folder and saw a picture of Gabriella leaving a market near her apartment. He knew the market well. That is where she did her grocery shopping. There was also a document that looked like a phone record. None of the numbers looked familiar to him. She only communicated with him, Jake, and Pac-Man. Nehemiah didn't believe this was her phone record.

"When you placed her in protective custody, you allowed us to monitor her activity. She bought a burner phone and called Montoya three times," Captain Jones informed the group.

"We need to question her as soon as possible," Mac said.

"She fled the safe house with her daughters." Captain Jones stared at Nehemiah.

"What is really going on here?" Nehemiah asked, feeling like he was being ambushed

"The evidence shows that your wife has not been forthcoming. We believe she has information in taking down Ortiz and his syndicate for good. Now, we need you to cooperate. Where is your wife?"

Nehemiah remembered the flash drive she had. There was something on the drive she was protecting, and until he knew what it was, he was keeping her whereabouts to himself. He was confident Jake wouldn't say anything, but there was no way Nehemiah was telling anyone else her location. Captain Jones may be the commanding officer of NCIS, but even he wasn't privy to the agency Nehemiah really worked for. Only other person in the room that knew was Mac, and he was being too quiet for his liking. Something else was going on, he could feel it.

"What do you mean where is she? Don't you have a detail on her? You have these pictures, you should have followed her, right?" Nehemiah figured if the Captain didn't know Gabriella's whereabouts, that meant no one in the room told him, and they also believed there was more to the story.

"She was able to ditch the detail, and we haven't seen her since." Captain Jones placed both hands on the table and stared Nehemiah in the eyes. "You mean to tell me she hasn't tried to contact you?"

"I last talked to my wife three months ago and she was safe in Indianapolis, but you know that. If my wife ran, she must have believed her life was in danger. She is smart and will surface when she is ready."

"Petty Officer Bolden, I don't have to tell you that if you are not being truthful, I will find out. There will be consequences to pay." The captain turned to the other two men in the room. "You will all pay." He stormed from the room, slamming the door behind him.

No one said a word. Mac motioned to the phone in the middle of the table. Jake then stood up and gave Nehemiah the sign that meant "follow me in 10 minutes." Nehemiah nodded his head in understanding. Once Jake left the room, Mac said, "Bolden, if you know something, now is the time to say something." While he was talking, Mac wrote "rat tag" on a notepad, indicating there was a listening device in the room and probably surveillance would be following them.

"Mac, I don't know where she is, but I'm going to find out."

The two men stood, shook hands, exchanging a cellular sim card between their palms. Nehemiah left the room first and headed straight for the parking lot. Mac stayed back, undoubtedly, to gather more information.

Once in his car, Nehemiah spotted Jake's car at the exit. He followed behind him at a safe distance. Twenty minutes later, they pulled up to a Waffle House on Atlantic Blvd, near Interstate 295. Before Nehemiah exited his car, he removed his phones SIM card and destroyed it, replacing it with the one Mac had just given to him.

The two men sat at the counter a few seats apart, neither saying a word to the other. They ordered their food and silently waited. The waitress was an older lady, with grey hair pulled tightly into a bun and covered with a hairnet. She moved swiftly across the kitchen floor, taking orders and serving food. She placed two plates of eggs and bacon in front of Nehemiah and Jake. After about five minutes, she gave each of them a bill and placed it face down on the counter.

Without looking, Nehemiah left a $20 bill on the counter and walked away, taking the handwritten check with him. Jake did the same. The receipt had the location and time of where to meet Mac. This was a system they had put into place for times of discretion such as this. The waitress was an undercover agent in their unit.

The Twelve Mile Swamp Conservation area was a few miles from a highly populated shopping area in St. Augustine, FL. The men parked their vehicles at various places and walked to the conservation area. The swamp was dense forestry, and they would be able to talk freely.

Jake arrived just after Nehemiah. They walked further into the trees to ensure obscurity from the road.

"Jake! What the hell is going on? Did you know any of that?" Nehemiah asked.

"Absolutely not. I would have never let you walk into an ambush like that. I'm not even sure why I was asked to be there."

"Well, I don't like it. There is something else going on. I'm sure of it. Captain Jones didn't even know Gabriella's whereabouts. That has to mean there was no detail around her."

Mac found them deep in the trees. "Could you have stayed a little closer to the road. It was a long walk to get out here."

"Come on, Mac, you run 18-20 miles every morning before breakfast. You're in better shape than us."

"Speak for yourself. I'm in great shape," Jake joked.

Mac informed them that Captain Jones was not completely working in the best of interest of the United States. Someone under the Captain's command was able to warn Gabriella to run, which is why she left Indianapolis. That person had not been identified yet. Nehemiah was correct in his assumption that Gabriella didn't have a security detail any longer. They had been pulled from watching her two months ago.

Captain Jones was also heading a task force targeting child trafficking; except they haven't had any good intel, until recently. Carlos Montoya surfaced at a Puerto Rican resort with a new wife who happens to also be the head of housekeeping. He was using the same ruse he had with Gabriella nearly 8 years ago.

"I guess Carlos decided to get back into the game," Jake said.

"But why now, after all of these years?" Nehemiah asked.

"I don't know, and I don't care. Bolden, I need you to go back in," Mac told him.

It may have sounded like a request, but it was a command when it came from Mac. No matter how Nehemiah felt, he knew he had to do this before he retired. Taking down Ortiz for the last time and making sure his wife lived without fear was his priority.

"One last question. Why is Jake involved?"

Mac laughed. "Jake has been recruited to be a civilian member of the unit. We didn't want to tell you until you retired. But it looks like we don't have a choice now."

"Welcome to the team." Nehemiah gave him a bear hug. Even though he would be retired, he would still have ties to the unit. They were like a second family.

Chapter 5

Scott was preparing to go out for an evening run through the neighborhood. He was still living in Moses and Neiko's condo while they were in Atlanta. Looking for a job was time-consuming, and he was not any closer to finding employment that he truly had a passion for.

The military was supposed to be short-term; enlist, get his educational benefits, and get out. After serving for 20 years, Scott realized he enjoyed serving his country more than he had initially thought. Now, he was trying to find something as comparable and fulfilling.

He walked into the kitchen, intending to get an apple to munch on before he went out. Instead, he sat at the breakfast bar and started daydreaming about Rachel. She was different from the women he had been in relationships within his past. Typically, Scott sought out non-military women; only once had he dated another servicemember. He liked his women to have some substance about them, but after a few dates, he was bored with them. None of them seemed to have enough drive, grit or passion for their futures.

Rachel had those three qualities, as well as, others. She was also different from what he thought an entertainment and music mogul would be like. When he first met Elijah, it was nothing like he imagined. Monica had gotten him tickets to an Evolution concert. His tickets included a pre-show meet and greet, and VIP passes.

Scott was amazed that on stage, he was Evolution, but before and after performances, he was just Elijah Bolden. The meet and greet was so relaxed and calm; nothing like he envisioned. Scott thought it would be screaming fans and tons of security. Instead, people were walking around eating walking tacos out of Doritos bags, and Elijah was engrossed in a game of spades with two fans and the drummer of his band.

Everyone in the Bolden family was not what he expected. So why would Rachel be any different? She ate Coney dogs like the girl next door and was very humbled. She wasn't one for flaunting her accolades, status, or wealth. If Scott had to give what he was feeling a name, it would be…admiration.

He took the last bite of his apple and grabbed a bottle of water from the refrigerator. The buzz from the intercom startled him. While walking to the wall unit to find out who was buzzing him, it started again, and then, a voice boomed through.

"Scott! Scott are you there?"

"Yes, Rachel, I'm here."

"Are you busy? I need a favor," she asked.

"Sure. Do you need me to come over there or are you coming over here?"

"I'll come over there. Bye."

Scott laughed thinking about how similar Rachel was to Monica. They were both the baby girls of the family and spoiled by their brothers. Not with material things, but with love. He began walking toward the door to wait for Rachel when he heard her coming down the stairs. He had forgotten that she had a key and the rooftop pool had an entrance to each condo.

She was dressed in her professional best. An all-black pantsuit tailored just for her figure, complemented by a pair of red leather stilettos. Scott couldn't help but imagine this boss in the boardroom or sitting behind her desk throwing commands at her staff. The truth is, he knew she wasn't the type to intimidate people with her power. Rachel would rather get down in the trenches with her people than stand by and watch.

"Hey Scott, I need some help this evening. I'm attending an event where I will need security. I hate having bodyguards and security details. If you're not busy, could you escort me? It's not formal, but you will need to wear a suit. It's an awards ceremony, and I hope to be in and out in less than three hours." Before Scott could give her an answer, she continued to talk. "I'll understand if you are not interested or if you're busy. I know it's last minute, but it never hurts to ask."

Scott watched the self-assured, confident businesswoman change to a vulnerable and unsure woman. She fidgeted with her hands for a few moments before straightening her spine and staring at him, awaiting an answer. He wanted to answer her before her nervousness had her talking again.

He gently clasped her small hands in his much larger and calloused ones. "Rachel, I would love to go," he said. "What time do I need to be ready?" Scott felt her relax and exhale. She closed her eyes briefly before looking up at him. He hadn't noticed before, but her eyes had flections of green in the caramel coloring.

"Scott, you are a lifesaver. You don't understand how much pressure and strain it is to be a top executive in this industry and to despise the constant media attention. It's very overwhelming to be a homebody and introvert like me."

"Introvert, really? I would have never taken you for an introvert."

"I put on a good front, but being around lots of people just drains me, and I have to be alone for periods of time to re-energize myself. The only exception is my family. I can be around all of them and be the happiest ever." She paused to think about her family and about Nehemiah and his current situation. "Well, can you be ready about 7 PM?"

Scott glanced at his watch and saw that it was 5PM already. He wouldn't need much time to get ready. His suits were fresh from the dry-cleaners, and all he would need to do is shower and get dressed. "I can be ready."

Her eyes danced a little before she walked away, this time choosing to exit from the front door and not the way she came…through the pool. Rachel paused with her hand on the doorknob. Scott thought she was going to turn and ask another favor. Instead, she opened the door and softly closed it behind her.

Scott stood there for a few moments after Rachel left thinking about the lifestyle that everyone around him lived. They were rich, successful, and famous. He wondered if that was a life, he could grow accustomed to. The Boldens expertly handled situations that happened around them, but to constantly live in the public eye had to be daunting.

*****

Rachel quickly walked to her condo and ran to her prayer room. She was having impure thoughts about Scott and wasn't sure how to process them. This man, who had just come into her life a few weeks ago, was causing her to have lustful thoughts, and she knew that had to be a sin.

Her prayer room was the walk-in closet in the third bedroom of her condo. The closet was the size of an average sized bedroom. She wasn't the type to have an abundance of clothes and shoes. Most didn't believe that as a wealthy, single woman in the entertainment industry, she didn't have designer items flowing from every room. Rachel loved to shop, but she usually replaced items instead of holding on to closets full of things she may never wear again.

Rachel opted for beautiful and functional. That was how she was raised. Her mother raised seven children on a military salary, which was not the easiest thing to do. Being thrifty and smart with money was how her family was able to be where they currently were financially. Good investments also helped.

The walls of her prayer room were covered in scriptures and motivational quotes. In one corner, were several plush pillows and a blanket. The room also had a small table with her laptop, bible, notebooks for taking notes, and candles. Rachel loved the smell of candles while she prayed and studied her Bible. Her room was a place of peace, quiet, solitude, hope, and faith. Whenever she was in her prayer room, she had clarity and discernment. She always felt the presence of God when she was in there.

Security was also important to her peace of mind, so her prayer room also doubled as a safe room. The room was designed by Nehemiah and included a two-person authentication passcode safe, a communication intercom, video surveillance of all four condos, and a secret passage to the safe room in Elijah's condo. Once activated, both safe rooms would lock down and immediately alert the police. The only way to open the safe room door from the outside after activation was to have someone enter the entry code on the outside, and the person on the inside had to enter another code.

Nehemiah also made sure the rooms were packed with water and non-perishable food. There was even a separate ventilation system for both rooms. He tried to think of everything when he designed the rooms.

Rachel sat on the floor of her prayer room and cried. She rocked back and forth trying to pray to God, but her emotions were jumbled and taking over. Clutching her Bible to her chest, she just repeated "Jesus, Jesus, Jesus," over again. Finally, the tears subsided. Rachel wanted to call her mother but wasn't ready for a lecture. She opted to call her sister. Naomi answered on the first ring.

"Hey, little lady. what's up?"

"Are you busy?" Rachel sniffled.

"Rachel, have you been crying? What's wrong? What happened?"

"I need to talk. Do you have time?"

"For my sister? Of course, I do. I'm walking to my bedroom now." Naomi tossed out directions to her children as she made her way to her bedroom to talk uninterrupted.

"Okay, talk to me."

Rachel didn't know where to start. She felt so bad for her thoughts, and she couldn't concentrate enough to find God's word on the matter. "Naomi, I've been having strange feelings around men. No, not men, just Scott."

"Monica's brother, Scott? He is so cute."

"Be serious, please. I don't know what to do. One minute, I'm looking at him like a juicy cheeseburger and the next minute I'm running to my prayer room, asking for forgiveness of my lustful thoughts."

"Rachel, have you never had these feelings for any other men before?"

"No," Rachel declared.

"Of all of the men you are around daily. At the studio, jet-setting across the country, industry events, you have never been attracted to another man?"

"How many ways do I have to say it? No! I've never felt this before. Sure, I thought a guy to be attractive. Even been on a few dates, but nothing like this. Scott is more than handsome."

"But you dated that guy for like a year. What's his name?"

"Stop playing games; you know his name. Franklin. And, no. Not anything close to the vibes I get with Scott."

"Wow. Let me take this in for a minute. My baby sister may be in love," Naomi teased.

"Forget it, I'm calling Mom. I would rather have her lecture to me than to have you make fun of me."

"Wait, let me call her. I want to hear what she has to say."

Naomi quickly connected their call with their mother. Jaclyn was more than knowledgeable about the situation. She raised her children effortlessly, and counseled many other parents, she would know what to do and say. So, when Jaclyn answered the phone, Naomi quickly filled her mother in on everything Rachel had told her and added her own opinions as well.

"When you think about him, do you get a little jolt up your spine? Does he make you smile, even when there is nothing funny? Am I getting this right?" Jaclyn asked.

"Yes, Mother," Rachel replied.

"Attraction is a good thing. What you are feeling is not lust. Lust is when you act on your attraction before marriage, but let's talk about the right now. You had lunch with him a few days ago, and tonight you two are going out, again."

Rachel quickly interrupted, "Yes, but to an awards ceremony. It's not a date. I asked him to escort me because I didn't want Marco or one of the other security guys hanging around me all night."

"Keep telling yourself that's why you asked him," Naomi interjected.

"Honey, just go and have fun. This is the fun part of getting to know someone. If you keep having these feelings, pray to God for understanding and discernment."

"Thank you, Mother."

"I love you, Rachel. And, next time you need advice, call Ruth. Naomi fell in love with the first man who told her she was cute."

Naomi giggled and said, "And, we've been together ever since. Love you, Sis. Love you, Mom."

Rachel laughed at her mother and sister when she disconnected the call. They kept her grounded and sane in times when she didn't know which way to go. She stayed in her closet and focused on her prayers. Her mother was right. She could look, just don't touch.

*****

Nehemiah made it to Miami in just under three hours. The family had a secure phone line to their parents' home located in Elijah's condo. He hated to intrude on his brother and his family at this time of the evening, but it was important to talk to Gabriella as soon as possible.

The babies were letting the entire floor know they were awake as soon as Nehemiah got off the elevator. He inwardly smiled, remembering the day Tierra was born. He had arrived at St. Vincent's Women's Hospital just in time for his princess to make her arrival. That moment, holding his tiny daughter in his arms, changed his entire world.

The door to Condo Calvary opened, causing Nehemiah to jerk and prepare to attack.

"Sorry, dude. I didn't know you were out here," Scott said.

"My bad, Scott. I'm a little jumpy with everything going on."

"Yeah, I understand. Let me know what I can do to help."

"Actually, if you have some time, I do need your help."

"Anything. What is it?"

"Let's go into the maternity ward over here," he pointed toward Condo Alpha where Elijah and his family lived. Nehemiah knocked on the door a few times before it opened.

"Come on in." Elijah was holding his son in one hand, trying to balance the bottle with his chin, and holding a stinky diaper in his other hand.

"Bro, warn someone before you allow them to enter into that stink. What does that baby eat to make him smell that way?"

"Stop acting like you haven't done this before."

"At least Tierra's poop smelled like roses. My daughter was a perfect baby."

"I'm sure Gabriella would say otherwise." Elijah motioned for them to have seat. "What do I owe this pleasure?"

"We need to use the secure line to Dad's."

"Everything okay? Anything else the family needs to know about?"

"Your family? No! I'm not giving the family any more information," Nehemiah exclaimed. He was not happy that he had to involve any one in the family, including his parents.

Elijah nodded his head in the direction of his office. "Feel free to use it. Karyn and I will be in the babies' room if you need either of us."

"Thanks, Bro." Nehemiah and Scott went into his brother's office and closed the door. "Scott, have you ever thought about a job in security?"

"Actually, I've been thinking about where I belong in this new civilian world. I know I need to work; this retirement check ain't nearly enough. And, I'm skilled at security, but I'm not settling for some night watchman or flashlight cop type of job. That's just not me."

Nehemiah laughed. With the military career Scott had, he understood not wanting to be a flashlight cop or anything. Nehemiah was thinking more along the lines of working for his security company.

"The pay is great, the hours suck, but it's easy work for someone of your caliber. Sometimes we get called to cases that are much more than just being a bodyguard for a celebrity or politician. Give it some thought. I'd love to have you on board."

Nehemiah called his father on the secure line. It didn't take long for his father to answer. Nehemiah explained what he had found out and asked to speak with Gabriella. A few minutes later, Gabriella was on the line.

"Gabriella, I need you to give my father the flash drive. It's important. I also need to ask you about making phone calls out in public. The government has photos of you.

"Nehemiah, I promise to you that I did not make any calls outside of the apartment. When we left during the day, we followed the protocol every time. We kept our heads down, we didn't talk to anyone, and we always returned within two hours."

"I believe you, baby. Nothing is adding up, and I need that information."

Nehemiah waited while Gabriella gave the information to his father. Jeremiah came back on the line and audibly exhaled, "Son, the information is coming through now. Whew! It's a doozy."

The flash drive consisted of names of high-power politicians in the United States and abroad who have been customers of Montoya's. There were detailed lists of who and what they purchased. Carlos Montoya kept meticulous records that would come back to bite him in the butt, and he had no idea.

Jeremiah transferred the files to an encrypted file and returned the bracelet to Gabriella. She was instructed not to trust anyone who wasn't family, Jake, or Scott. Not anyone in the government, either.

Nehemiah was heading into the Miami Divine office to get the encrypted file that his father sent to him. "Scott, you are welcome to come with me. Check out the office set-up, review our client lists…"

"Thanks, but I'm escorting Rachel to an event tonight. I really should be getting ready right now. Don't want to be late."

"Oh, you're going on a date with my sister." It was said as a statement and not a question. Nehemiah's demeanor changed from colleague and friend to intimidating big brother.

"Not a date," Scott clarified. She didn't want a security detail following her all evening."

"Yeah, that's what she said. Listen, my sister is young and impressionable. She is a little green when it comes to men and relationships. Don't give me a reason to have to 'talk' to you. Do you understand?"

"Being a big brother myself, I completely understand."

Chapter 6

Nehemiah remained in Elijah's office after Scott left. He needed to confide in his brother, but he didn't want to put Elijah's family in any jeopardy. Knowing too much about the situation might cause a problem, and Nehemiah did not want to take that risk.

Yet, if he didn't talk things through with someone, he might find himself on the wrong side of the battle. He walked into Elijah's kitchen, which was identical to the other condos. Nehemiah went straight for the apple juice he knew that his brother always kept in the refrigerator.

He smiled at the baby video monitor on the kitchen counter. Safety first; and nothing but the best for Elijah's twins. He wondered if he said something aloud, would they be able to hear him.

"If you're not too busy, can you meet me in the kitchen?" he spoke.

Nehemiah didn't have to wait long before his brother appeared.

"Where are the babies?" he asked Elijah.

"The twins are asleep, and Karyn tries to stay on their schedule, so she just dozed off, too. You look worried, what's up, brother?"

The brothers had an unbreakable bond that went back to Nehemiah's teenage years. There was a seven-year difference between them, but Nehemiah always felt closer to his younger brother.

Their bond became stronger one spring, when Nehemiah had been playing basketball alone in the backyard. The ball bounced over the fence into the neighbor's yard. Nehemiah jumped the fence to retrieve his ball and overheard yelling coming from the house.

The neighbors kept to themselves, rarely interacting with anyone else. Nehemiah had seen the wife a few times, but never spoke to her. The kids around the neighborhood had started a rumor that the house was haunted, and the wife was a ghost.

He went closer toward the house to find out if he could hear more. The husband was shouting and throwing things. Nehemiah thought he heard the wife screaming for help. He was raised to help people in need, so he was unable to walk away. So, Nehemiah knocked on the door. When there was no answer, he tried to open the door, and to his surprise, it opened.

He was trying to formulate a plan for what he intended to do when he found the couple. He made his way through the kitchen and living room to find lots of broken items. Nehemiah kept following the screaming voices upstairs to the couple's bedroom. As soon as he got to the top of the steps, the husband came out of the room.

"Who the hell are you?" he shouted.

"I heard screaming and I came over to help," Nehemiah responded.

"Help who? That whore in there?"

Nehemiah had never heard a man talk to his wife in that manner. His father had never raised his voice at his mother, and neither had any of his uncles with their wives. He wanted to respond but couldn't. The man towered over his scrawny 5'8" frame and stood right in front of him. Without warning, the man pushed Nehemiah into the wall.

"You want to help? You can't even help yourself," he growled.

Nehemiah was in shock that this man had pushed him against the wall. The man took a step back and, then, raised his hand. The scene seemed like it was moving in slow-motion when Nehemiah saw the wife step out of the room with a black eye, busted lip, and covered in blood. That was all it took for Nehemiah to jump into action.

Instead of cowering at the thought that this grown man was about to hit him, he stepped up and threw his fist into the side of the man's face. He caught the man off guard, and he stumbled backward before falling to the ground. Nehemiah was so enraged, he jumped on top of the man and alternated punches…left, then right, and left, again.

He cried and punched until he felt himself being pulled off the man.

"You ain't a man, you're a punk. Hitting on women and kids. You're a punk!" Nehemiah shouted.

Nehemiah was outside when he realized it was the mailman and a 10-year-old Elijah who had pulled him off the lifeless man. The postman told them to run home and not say anything to anyone. He said he would take care of things, and not to worry.

When the boys arrived home, they both went to the bedroom they shared and cried. Nehemiah was angry, and Elijah was scared. Together, they decided to keep the secret and not ever mention what happened to anyone.

They never found out what happened after they ran home. The next day, the neighbor's house was empty. The couple had moved out in the middle of the night. And, Elijah and Nehemiah never spoke of that day.

But it was at that time when Nehemiah and Elijah really grew close. They had a secret that no one knew about, and one they would never forget.

Nehemiah took a swig of his apple juice before answering his brother. "I'm worried. Now that everyone knows about Gabriella and the girls, I feel like I have a family that is real. Before, they were a secret; but now, everything I do, the family will be watching me."

"I hate to tell you, but your family was real before. You always did what needed to be done to take care of them. Even in Puerto Rico. I think you knew then that they were your family. Why else would you go to all of that trouble?" Elijah sat at the breakfast bar.

"But now, Mom and Dad know. And, Mom didn't react the way I thought she would. I was ready for almost anything, except that."

"Yeah, Mom has surprised me time and time, again."

The two brothers sat in silence for a few minutes. Each in their own thoughts.

"Do you ever think we should have told someone about that day?" Elijah asked.

"I used to. I sometimes wonder whatever happened to the woman. I hope she got away from her husband," Nehemiah replied.

"Do you think that maybe not knowing what happened to her is why you feel the pull to always help people, especially women?"

Nehemiah had never thought of that. He had stepped in with Neiko twice, and then, there was Chrystal. She was on his team, but he felt like she needed help. That was why her betrayal hurt so bad. He went out of his way to protect her.

"You know, brother, I might have to agree with your assessment," Nehemiah replied.

Chapter 7

Gabriella had been in the Bolden home for five days. It was refreshing to be able to go outside without worrying if anyone was watching her. And, as promised, Naomi brought her children over every day after school. Tiffany loved her new cousins. Tierra took some time warming up to them, but eventually joined into the fun. Gabriella also found that her mother-in-law was not anything like what she thought when they had first met.

She had to admit, she thought Jaclyn would hate her. Even when Nehemiah told her his mother wasn't that type of person, Gabriella assumed he was just trying to get her to be calm. From her experience, women were good at smiling while thinking the absolute worst of someone. But Gabriella quickly found out that Jaclyn was sincere and very loving.

Jaclyn treated her like a daughter and loved on her newest granddaughters, spoiling them rotten. She never overstepped her boundary as the grandmother; she still allowed Gabriella to be the mother and never made decisions without asking first. Gabriella had been concerned that Jaclyn's experience raising children would have her giving unsolicited advice about how to raise her daughters.

Their first day without Nehemiah, Gabriella tip-toed through the house as quiet as she could. She wanted to make breakfast for the family as a way of saying "thank you" for everything. Before the coffee pot could fill, Jeremiah walked into the kitchen, fully dressed for a day in the office, even though he was retired. He was dressed in black slacks and a white button shirt with no tie.

Jeremiah had already been to the gym, played several games of basketball, and was just returning home. Gabriella was startled when he entered from the garage door that led to a mudroom directly next to the kitchen.

"I'm sorry, Gabriella. I didn't mean to scare you," he said.

"I didn't expect anyone to be awake at this hour. Do you always go to work this early?"

He laughed a little at her confusion. "I don't work a traditional job anymore. I'm retired Navy."

"Oh, just like Nehemiah. He idolizes you." For the first time since she arrived and met her father-in-law, she took a good look at him. Nehemiah was so much like him. They had similar builds and beautiful, dark piercing eyes.

"I don't know about idolizing me," Jeremiah replied, as he reached into the refrigerator to get a bottle of cold water. "I certainly admire my son. Growing up, I thought he was the least likely of my sons to follow in my footsteps."

"Really!? You must tell me all about his childhood years. He is so quiet and rarely talks about his family or upbringing. I think it is because he didn't want me to feel bad for not being able to meet you all."

"Well, we're all glad to have finally met you. Sorry, it had to be under these circumstances." He walked over to Gabriella and kissed her forehead. "You and my granddaughters are beautiful, and I love you. I'm excited for you to be here."

Gabriella thought the elder Boldens were too good to be true. They were so accepting of her and her girls. She was waiting for something bad to happen, and so far, nothing but love poured from her new family.

Tiffany and Tierra loved their grandmother and grandfather. Spending quality time with them meant the world to the girls and Gabriella. She was amazed that Jaclyn and Jeremiah could make each grandchild feel special and loved. They had 21 grandchildren in total. Gabriella had only met Naomi's four children. Ruth and her six children were planning to return to Virginia in the upcoming weeks and couldn't wait to meet her and the girls.

"Mr. Bolden..."

Jeremiah interrupted her. "You can call me Jeremiah or Dad. None of that formal stuff. We are family."

She blushed a little before beginning again. "Dad...that sounds strange to me. I didn't have a father growing up. That is why it is important to me that the girls spend as much time with their father as possible."

"Were you raised in San Juan?" he asked.

"Actually, I grew up in Caguas, not far from San Juan. Graduated from Benitez High School before moving to San Juan with my mother." Gabriella lowered her head briefly thinking about her mother. "My mother was very sick when I left for college in the Virgin Islands. She didn't tell me she was sick. I came home to visit after my sophomore year, and she had been in the hospital. She wasn't going to tell me."

"As a parent, we always want to protect our children. I'm sure that her keeping her illness from you was not meant to hurt you, but to spare you from seeing her suffer," Jeremiah tried to comfort her.

"That's what she told me. She got better and was able to see me graduate from college. Then, died a few weeks later."

Jeremiah pulled her into a comforting hug. She trembled in his arms, realizing what she had missed not having a father around.

She stepped out of his embrace and wiped the tears from her eyes. "I'm sorry," she said.

"You have no reason to be sorry about anything."

Gabriella believed him. She had no reason to be sorry. It wasn't her fault her father left before she was born, and it wasn't her fault she was in this situation. She was fortunate to have bumped into Nehemiah that day in the hotel and grateful for the old woman at the market who told her to run from her husband and that Nehemiah was safe. Gabriella whole-heartedly believed God put Nehemiah in front of her to save her and Tiffany from the horror they were experiencing.

"Dad, would you like something to eat? I was going to prepare breakfast for everyone."

"That sounds wonderful. What are we having?" Jaclyn asked upon entering the kitchen.

Gabriella smiled. This was her chance to introduce her culture to her in-laws. "I was thinking about arroz con leche and tortilla de huevos. That's a type of sweet rice and egg omelets."

Gabriella worked hard on breakfast as she participated in light conversation with Jeremiah and Jaclyn. Just as she was placing the last omelet in the warming dish, Tiffany walked into the kitchen rubbing her eyes. "Mama, I smelled food. Is that arroz con leche?"

The adults laughed at her. Jaclyn had just asked when the girls would awake. Gabriella knew the smell of food would draw Tiffany out of her slumber. She would have to wake Tierra, though. That girl could sleep through a tornado.

"Tierra sounds like Nehemiah. He was always late for school due to oversleeping past the alarm," Jaclyn smiled at the memory. "I remember having to chase him from the house with a broom and making him run for the school bus."

That got a laugh from everyone including Tiffany. "Did daddy get spankings when he was little?"

"Your dad was a wonderful child, who made some interesting decisions in life. I didn't need to spank him. I would look at him like this," Jaclyn made a face where she raised one eye brow and attempted to look mean. "And he would start crying."

Tiffany laughed again, at the face Jaclyn was making.

Jeremiah offered to wake Tierra and bring her to breakfast. The two of them had gotten closer the night before. Tierra hadn't wanted to play with the other children, but after the family meeting, Jeremiah was able to get her away from her father with a popsicle. Tierra was a little hesitant, but when Nehemiah told her it was okay, she opened up for her grandfather.

The family sat at the dining room table for breakfast, blessed their food, and began eating.

"This is just like on TV," Tiffany said.

"What's just like on TV?" Jaclyn asked.

"Eating at a big table with your family. The only person missing is Daddy." Tiffany lowered her head. "He had to go to work. He always leaves at night."

Gabriella's heart broke for her daughter. Tiffany would go through this somber mood for a while every time Nehemiah left them. She understood he had to go to work, but it didn't stop her from missing him.

"Tiffany, do you know what your father does at work?" Jeremiah asked.

"Yes. He defends the country to keep everyone safe, including us. He says it's dangerous, but he's good at it. And, when you're good at something, it doesn't feel like work. Daddy said that he found something else he is good at."

"Oh yeah? And, what is that?" Jaclyn asked.

"He said he's good at taking care of Mama and us girls, and he is good at loving us. That's what he wants to do forever."

Gabriella had to excuse herself from the table to gather her composure. She loved Nehemiah with all of her heart. The secrets and the hiding were starting to seriously affect her girls, and now she needed to protect them just like her husband does. In protecting them, she needed to set them all free.

She returned to the dining room to find the girls working on a puzzle with their grandparents. Gabriella's heart filled with so much love, respect, and admiration for her in-laws. They didn't have to accept her, and they certainly didn't have to allow her to live with them or protect her, but they did; and they didn't ask any questions.

A few day later, Gabriella was relaxing around the pool. Jaclyn had insisted she prepare the girls for bed and pretty much ordered her to relax. Jeremiah had been in his office for most of the day, only coming out to grab a snack and to have dinner with the family.

It was time Gabriella finished business in San Juan. It was time for her to go back and confront those demons. Before she left Indianapolis, she had purchased a couple of pre-paid cell phones. She had thought about this day for years. The time had come for her to finally put an end to everything. Carlos still had control over her life, and that ended now.

She left three envelopes on the table. One for the Boldens, one for the girls, and one for Nehemiah. The last two envelopes were only to be opened if she didn't return. Gabriella jumped into the pool fully dressed. The water would short-circuit any tracking devices that may have been in her clothing. She didn't put anything past Nehemiah.

Chapter 8

Scott was able to shower and dress in time to meet Rachel in the lobby of their building. He was casket-sharp, like the old people would say. Monica made him purchase the tailor-made Calvin Klein black suit a few years ago. He had never been a label type of guy, but he had to admit, the fit of the suit was perfect and felt good. He accented the suit with a red tie and matching pocket square.

He stepped off the elevator and saw Rachel talking with the doorman. She was radiant in the flowing red dress that stopped just above the knee. Her hair was done in big curls, swooped to one side in the back, secured with a sparkling hairpin. Scott lost his breath momentarily when she turned around and smiled at him.

Rachel was wearing a light amount of make-up. She was a natural beauty that didn't require any assistance. As he approached her, he saw she was also wearing diamond hoop earrings and a matching diamond bracelet around her wrist.

Scott maintained his eye contact with her and hugged her ever-so-gently. "You look absolutely stunning."

Rachel blushed at the compliment. "Thank you, Scott. Our transportation awaits us." She motioned toward the doors of the building. Waiting outside was a chauffeured black sedan, courtesy of Evolution Music.

The ride to the event was quiet. Scott was still in awe of the woman sitting beside him. He thought she was attractive the first time he met her at Karyn and Neiko's baby shower. The day they went to lunch, she reminded him of a young girl. She was dressed down in jeans and a flowing top. Earlier today, she looked like the company exec that she was, and now, she was all woman. It was best if he remembered Nehemiah's warning. The way his mind was wondering, he may forget.

They arrived at the W South Beach. Scott wasn't expecting the spectacle before him. Rachel had told him it was not formal, but from the look of the opulence, he wasn't so sure about that. The driver opened the door for him, and he walked around the car to assist Rachel from the vehicle. Once again, he noticed how small her hands were.

Scott had to force a smile on his face as they walked the red carpet. Rachel was used to the cameras and attention. She seemed very relaxed and in her element. He stood back and admired her presence. She worked the red carpet like a fashion model and spoke with class when answering questions for the media.

Once they entered the hotel, Scott felt the need to hold her hand; and she hadn't pulled away. She smiled at him; and that melted his heart. He had to quickly remember that he was also there in a security capacity. His focus needed to be on watching the surrounding area and people.

Before leaving the condo, Scott called Marco, the head of security for Elijah. He needed to know what to be aware of. Marco informed him that these types of events were mellow. Be aware of the drunkards and the men who thought they were above the law.

Fortunate for Scott, Rachel's reputation was easily seen as back-off. Her brothers had done a good job of warning any man who bothered her that they would have to deal with her brothers. People had a healthy fear of Moses and Elijah.

The ballroom was elegantly decorated with crystals and silver décor items at every table. The tables had white and silver table linens making the room appear sparkly. Lights reflected from every shiny surface. Even the centerpieces of white roses had crystals and glitter on them.

Rachel pulled Scott toward three gentlemen standing near one of the bars in the corner of the ballroom. She whispered to him, "These guys are a few of my artists."

"Hey, fellas!" Rachel greeted the group.

The three men turned at the sound of her voice. They each gave her a once over from head to toe, lingering too long for Scott's liking.

"Hey, Boss Lady. You looking good," the first guy said, completely ignoring Scott's presence. When she went to hug him, Scott held firmly to her hand, not wanting to let it go. She gave him a puzzled look before realizing she had not introduced him.

"I apologize. Scott, this is Taj, Kareem, and Nevins. They are signed to Evolution Records. Guys, this is Scott Heller, a friend of the family."

Scott was taller than each man by a few inches and had at least 30 lbs. on the bigger of the three. If they got out of line, he would gladly take them on.

He greeted each of them and participated in the light conversation, never releasing Rachel's hand. The action didn't go unnoticed by the men. They maintained their distance while conversing. She hadn't protested, either. He liked the feel of her hand in his. It felt right. Scott wondered if she felt the same way.

A waiter with a small chime came through the crowd. He walked around everyone hitting the chimes, which Scott realized meant it was time to be seated. Scott walked with Rachel toward their table, located at the front of the ballroom, right in front of the dais.

"I guess the really important people sit up front," Scott said, reaching for Rachel's chair.

"Something like that," she responded, with a smile.

The three guys from earlier were seated at their table along with an older gentleman and his date. Rachel introduced the gentleman as a vice president at Evolution Music. His date had to be thirty years younger than him. Scott hoped it was his daughter but was disappointed when the woman leaned over and kissed the man smack on the lips.

The ceremony started with a performance from a talented young woman he had never heard of. Scott had to admit, he wasn't current with pop culture. At least, now he knew the awards ceremony was for outstanding contributions in the community.

While dinner was being served, Scott got an uneasy feeling. He couldn't explain it, but something didn't seem right. He stayed observant while they ate and conversed with the others at their table.

*****

Rachel was enjoying her evening, unlike previous times at these types of events. Scott was handsome in his suit, and she had to concentrate on other things to stop herself from staring at him. She was glad she talked to her sister and mother earlier in the day. These crazy feelings she was having were natural. She had to keep telling herself that.

A few times at the table, she thought she saw Scott flash a jealous look at Taj and Kareem. Nevins was too busy flirting with the lady at the table next to them. She dismissed her assessment of Scott as not really knowing him that well. His expressions could have been innocent.

Scott hadn't seemed fazed by the celebrities in the room, that won him some points in her book. She found nothing more unattractive than a man who gets starstruck. She once dated a guy who couldn't stop talking about how he was sitting twenty feet away from Beyoncé.

The remainder of the ceremony was getting started, and she was preparing for the reaction from Scott and the others when her name was called for her award. She had gotten the call an hour before they arrived notifying her of the win.

The mistress of ceremony was a well-known and respected journalist in Miami. Her stage presence was powerful and commanded attention. Rachel turned her chair to face Scott. She wanted to see his reaction when her name was called.

"This year's recipient of the Woman of the Year in Community Engagement has been in her field and industry for a short time. Her family's foundation provides professional and leadership skills to young girls in the foster care system, along with music education in underserving school districts. She has personally facilitated several sessions on leadership development and discovering your passion. Every year, she has taken a group of young ladies to the Black Girls Rock convention in New York City, where they meet and learn from other women in a variety of different career fields. This year's recipient is the youngest to ever receive this award. I am excited to announce the 2019 Woman of the Year in Community Engagement, Rachel Bolden."

"You didn't tell me you were the winner," Scott said as she hugged him before taking the stage.

"I didn't know until we were almost here," she whispered to him.

Scott stood along with the rest of the room and celebrated her accomplishment. Rachel stood and gracefully walked the short distance from her table to the stage. All of a sudden, she was nervous. This wasn't the first award she had to receive over the past few years, but with Scott watching, her nerves started to go erratic.

She read her well-prepared acceptance speech. She hadn't known she would win, but she was prepared just in case. In her speech, she thanked her family, but especially, her brothers. They had been her support and driving force.

Rachel returned to the table and was stunned at the proud expression Scott displayed. She was falling too fast for a man she hadn't known long, and she felt like she needed to return to her prayer closet as soon as possible.

She had told Scott they would be in and out, but now she was fearing being alone with him on the ride home. Maybe she could tell him he could leave, and she would find a ride home with Taj or Kareem.

"Hey, I'm proud of you and your accomplishment," Scott told her.

"Thank you," Rachel said. "But her smile faltered a little before she was able to recover. Scott was very perceptive and noticed.

"Hey, what's wrong? Are you okay?"

"Yeah, I'm okay. I know I told you we would be in and out, but I am thinking about going to the after party. Seeing as I won and all, it's kind of expected. You don't have to stay. If you want to leave, I'm sure one of the guys can bring me home."

Scott stared at her and clenched his jaw which made Rachel uncomfortable. Surely, he couldn't be jealous. It's not like they were in a relationship or anything. They were just friends.

His features relaxed, and then, he flashed his smile at her. "I'd be happy to stay with you and attend the after-party. I'm in the presence of greatness." He, then, leaned forward and kissed her cheek.

Rachel felt her cheek go up in flames. The heat seeped right through her body. The feeling was so welcomed and disturbing at the same time. She wasn't sure how she was going to get through this after party with Scott beside her all evening. This was a bad idea.

The after-party event was being held on the rooftop of the hotel. The music was loud, and the crowd was thick. It seemed that everyone from the ballroom, plus a few extra 100 people, were on the roof. These were the times she hated the industry.

"Scott, I'm not feeling this. I will just show my face around, speak to a few people and we can get out of here."

He replied, "No problem."

Rachel circulated through the crowd. Several entertainers, athletes, and local celebrities were in attendance. As she took a step or two, there was someone congratulating her on her win and her accomplishments. A few people she knew, and some she didn't, had wanted to take pictures with her. She had gotten good at politely exiting conversations. After laughing at a few jokes from one of her colleagues, she excused herself and continued to mingle throughout the room.

Once she felt she had talked to the required people, she turned to Scott and said, "That's it. I'm done. Let's get out of here."

Scott called their driver and they headed for the elevator. Their escape was almost flawless, until they were approached by a drunken wannabe rapper. The man had been trying to get the attention of every producer and agent on the roof.

"Hey girl, why you leaving so soon? I ain't get a chance to talk to you about my new music." He was slurring his words so badly, Rachel was barely able to understand him.

"Contact my office. Someone will get back to you," Rachel replied.

"Why I gotta call your office if you right here?" he asked, stepping closer to her. Scott was able to effectively block him from getting closer.

"The lady asked you to call her office. Back up," he said, firmly.

"Who is you?" the guy asked, as he stumbled back a step.

Rachel was afraid Scott would cause a scene. That was the last thing she needed. She tried to signal for party security to intervene. They arrived too late. Scott had the guy by his collar up against the elevator door.

"Scott, let him go. You are making a scene," she pleaded.

Scott never made a sound. He didn't yell or anything but the way he was holding the guy at his throat, lifted him a few inches from the ground and was cutting off his air. Party security arrived and had to pry Scott's fingers from the guy. "We got it from here, Sir. Ma'am, we apologize."

The fury that was emanating from Scott could be felt from everyone around. When the elevator arrived, the other guests let them enter alone, opting to wait for another elevator. When the doors closed, Rachel ripped into him.

"How dare you embarrass me in front of the people I have to work with? I have never been so humiliated. Marco never would have never done anything like that."

"Then, why didn't you ask Marco to come with you?"

Rachel could tell he was still angry but was trying to calm down. He never raised his voice, but if looks could kill, she would be dead three times over. Instead of answering him, she turned her back to him and waited until the elevator arrived in the lobby level.

The doors opened, and Scott pulled her in the opposite direction of the exit. She tried to pull away from him, but his grip was too tight. Rachel was concerned when he stopped in a secluded area. She was just as angry as he was at the moment.

In a whisper, Scott began, "You asked me to accompany you as security. And, as such, it is my responsibility to keep you safe. What did you think I would do?" When she didn't immediately answer, he continued. "You wanted to show me your world. Show me how these men fall over themselves for you. Great...got it...I see it now, and I want no part of your world."

"You don't know anything about my world. Those men don't want me, they want what I can offer them by way of fame and fortune." Rachel tried to hold back her tears.

Scott appeared to calm down and blew out a deep breath. "Let's get you home." He walked her back toward the front of the hotel where their sedan was waiting. He opened her door and helped her inside.

Rachel waited for Scott to enter on the other side, but when the driver got in and pulled off, she became confused. "Wait, where is Scott?"

"He said he would find another way home," the driver responded.

This time she let the tears fall. She couldn't understand what made him so mad. She was the one who should be angry. He embarrassed her in front of others by almost choking that guy. He should have let security handle things. Then, she thought about it. He wasn't used to these types of events. He was a military guy; and if Nehemiah had been there, the guy would be in the back of an ambulance right now.

She had to call her mother, again. This wasn't how she saw her evening going; and now she didn't know what to do next.

Chapter 9

Scott walked toward Collins Park and found a bench where he could sit and think. He needed time to understand what his feelings toward Rachel were. He was somewhere between intrigued and nervous. This wasn't how he had felt with any other woman, yet Rachel and all her naivete was able to unnerve him and awaken a passion within him that he didn't know existed.

While he sat there on the bench, watching people go on with their lives, he wondered what was in store for his life. He was in Miami to relax and figure out where to go from here. He hadn't thought about staying here. Or could he? No sooner than the thought of staying in Miami crossed his mind, his cell phone rang. He checked the caller ID, first, and noticed it was Ric calling. Scott quickly prayed everything was okay with his sister.

"What's up, Ric?"

"I heard you were looking for work," said Ric.

"Something like that. What did you have in mind?"

"How about the head of security for Diaz, Inc.? My current security chief announced his retirement this morning. With the way things are going on around here, and the possible expansion, I was hoping you would want the job."

Scott had heard people say, "God was an on-time God," and this moment was his proof of that. His brother-in-law couldn't have picked a better time to call.

"I think I might like that."

"Perfect. When can you get to Atlanta? You can start immediately. You understand you would be overseeing security operations for the Atlanta and Detroit locations, as well as our expansion?" Ric asked.

Scott didn't take any time to mull over the position. He willingly accepted. "Sounds like a task I'm ready for. I appreciate you thinking of me."

"Come on, Scott, you're my brother. Family looks out for one another, at all times."

They chatted for a few minutes before Ric had to take care of some other business. Scott agreed to being in Atlanta the next day. He didn't have much to pack up in the condo, so he could be on the road in about two hours.

That just left him having to tell Rachel goodbye. He hated to admit that he would miss her, but he needed to be away from her for a while. The feelings she evoked within him were new and foreign to him, and he needed time to process everything.

Scott caught an Uber back to the condos. He decided to wait until he was leaving to talk to Rachel. After packing all his things, he called Neiko to let her know he would be joining her in Atlanta. Of course, she already knew, and welcomed him to the Diaz work family.

He did a final look around the condo, taking in the beauty and opulence of the space and making sure that he didn't leave anything behind. Carrying three large bags, he backed out of the front door and bumped right into Rachel. Scott could see she had been crying. He wanted to reach out to her, but instinctively knew she would back away.

She had changed into her comfortable sweatpants and t-shirt

and removed her make-up. Her beauty was natural and effortless. Some women tried too hard to get the same glow and attractiveness Rachel genuinely had.

"You're leaving?" she asked. He could feel the heat from her question.

Adjusting his bags on his shoulder. "Yeah, Ric offered me a job at Diaz in Atlanta," he said.

"Just like that? Didn't Nehemiah also offer you a job at his company?"

"Look, Rachel. All of this entertainment, celebrity stuff is a little too fast for my taste. I'm just a D-town guy. Apparently, from tonight, I'm not cut-out for personal security." He wanted to tell her he wasn't cut out to be *her* personal security. Too many feelings were in play.

"I see," she replied, looking down at her feet. "Well, I wish you luck in your new job."

"Rachel," he said on an exhale. When she looked up at him, his heart took a dip and had to swallow hard to get past the lump in his throat. "I'm a phone call away. I'll see you at the next family function."

"Yeah, whatever," she said.

Scott hated seeing her like this. He felt like he was breaking her heart or something. They had never been on a real date; they hadn't even talked about dating each other. A few lunch outings didn't establish a relationship. Or did it to her? At this moment, one thing was for certain to Scott…he had to leave before he got in too deep with her.

He stepped forward and kissed her forehead. "Be safe, boss lady." Without looking back, he entered the elevator and walked away from her. Scott told himself on the ride to the lobby, it had to be this way.

*****

Rachel returned to her prayer closet and called her sister, again. She felt humiliated all over again. The first time she felt more than a friendship for a man, and he walked away from her. She couldn't blame Scott. He didn't feel the same way about her as she had for him. She was the one with the crush, not him. He was a man who probably had plenty of women in his life. She was the one who had no romantic involvements.

The call to her sister didn't help much, but it was comforting to hear that her sister had been through similar situations before meeting and falling in love with her husband. Nevertheless, Rachel remained in her closet for a few hours until she eventually fell asleep on the floor.

The next morning, Rachel awoke to find a text message from Scott. He was the last person she thought she would hear from. The message simply said that he had made it safely to Atlanta. She smiled at his consideration in letting her know he was safe. She didn't want to read more into the gesture.

Rachel tried to put Scott behind her; completely out of her mind. She took a shower, dressed, and prepared for her day like she would any other day. It was Saturday morning, and with no appointments on the calendar, she decided to check in on her brother, Elijah, and his growing family. The twins had been home for a couple of weeks, and Rachel couldn't wait until she could spoil them rotten.

Instead of going to the front door of Elijah's condo and knocking like most people would do, she decided to go through the pool entrance, where she didn't need to knock. Her family was used to her barging into their homes.

From the pool deck, Rachel could see her brother in the kitchen. Great, she thought. She was just in time for breakfast.

"Hello, Brother. What's cooking?"

"Cook for yourself. I have just about 45 minutes to eat and spend time with my wife before one of the babies or Jaleel wakes up. Bye," said Elijah, as he kissed her cheek and ran from the kitchen carrying a plate full of scrambled eggs and bacon.

Rachel thought the couple was cute and very much in love. She wanted that; the love that each of her siblings shared with their spouses. She wanted to know what it felt like to be the center of a man's attention, but not just any man; a man she loved, and who loved her back, unconditionally.

She didn't make breakfast. Instead, she grabbed an apple and returned to the pool area. Rachel stared at the sky, looking for God to send her a signal, a message, or anything letting her know she would eventually find a husband and have a love life. She was a patient woman, but how much more patient did she need to be?

Laughter from Karyn broke into her thoughts. Rachel smiled, her siblings were truly blessed with the spouses they had. She returned into Elijah's condo for another apple when she heard soft whimpering through the baby monitor. She thought it could be the babies and went to the nursery to check on them. Sure enough, little Erica was waking up.

Rachel didn't want Erica to wake her brother, so she picked her up from the crib, grabbed a diaper, some wipes, and a baby bottle of water before quietly exiting the nursery. She was an old pro at taking care of babies. Rachel clocked more babysitting hours than some day care workers.

As Rachel was changing Erica's diaper in the living room, she dreamed of one day having her own children, but first, she needed a husband. The thoughts of Scott came flooding back to her mind. What would their children look like?

"Hey girl, you didn't have to do that," Karyn said, walking into the living room, tying the belt of her robe around her waist.

"No problem. Auntie Rachel was here to save the day," Rachel kissed all over her niece. "Have you talked to Neiko? Isn't she due to give birth soon?"

"Neiko is overdue by a week. Her doctors scheduled to induce her next week. We are going to see her in Atlanta. Did you want to come?"

"Is it safe for the babies to travel?"

"We are planning to drive. I don't think they need to be flying just yet."

Rachel thought about going to Atlanta for a few minutes. She would be able to see Scott, again, but then again, he was the one who left. They weren't a couple, so Rachel wasn't sure why she felt this way. They had lunch a couple of times and went to one event, and now, she was feeling possessive and territorial.

She wanted to decline the invitation but found she couldn't. "Yes, I will ride with you guys. Please tell me Elijah is not driving?" The two women laughed, knowing that Elijah tended to drive faster than the flow of traffic.

"I heard that, you two," Elijah said through the baby monitors.

Rachel wanted to talk. She needed to talk about her feelings for Scott. She had gotten Christian advice from her mother, and sisterly advice from Naomi, but now she wanted the dirty truth. Karyn wouldn't hold back and would tell it to her straight.

"Is there anywhere in this house that doesn't have a nanny cam or baby monitor?"

"The pool deck. We can go out there and talk if you need to."

Chapter 10

"What do you mean you lost the tracking signal?" Nehemiah roared into the phone.

"Exactly what I said. I got the notification that it wasn't signaling anymore," Jake informed him.

Nehemiah was more than infuriated at the moment. How had the tracking signal been discovered? Jake was very good at placing the small device in locations that were difficult to find. All her clothing items and shoes had been placed with a device. Then, it occurred to him that maybe she knew she was being tracked.

He was questioning all her past actions and conversations. Were there any signs that she knew or would do something like this? She had already given all the information from the bracelet to his father, what else was there to be done? She was safe at the Bolden home, so what was she thinking?

It had to be something huge to leave the girls and run away. Didn't she think she could come to him or Jake? He had to call his dad and find out what he knew.

"Let me call my dad." Nehemiah ended the call and dialed his parents' house.

Jeremiah answered on the first ring. "Son, I just found out Gabriella is gone. She left some letters for you and the girls by the pool. She couldn't have been gone more than 30 minutes. I just checked the security cameras. She jumped in the pool fully dressed, and then, ran toward the trees behind the house."

So, she did know about the devices and deliberately disabled them. Nehemiah had no idea what was going on with Gabriella. She couldn't possibly think it was a good idea to go after Carlos alone. Unless, there was something she was hiding. He had to get to her before she did something stupid.

The last thing he wanted was for his daughters to lose both of their parents. Nehemiah had to find her. He called Jake and informed him of what was going on. He, then, went straight to the airport for the next flight to San Juan, knowing that was where she would be heading to.

While waiting for an available flight, Nehemiah found out more information from Mac about some things happening in Puerto Rico, and with Ortiz. There was a DEA task force on the ground in Puerto Rico, operating from the old Roosevelt Roads Naval Base.

He wasn't interested in working on any joint task force. All he cared about was finding his wife and making sure she stayed safe. Mac mentioned their unit had not been officially called in to assist, but with him on the ground in San Juan, he should be available if they needed him.

The two-and-a-half hour flight to San Juan seemed more like two days to Nehemiah. He teetered between rage and fear. Gabriella had to know what she was doing to him. For the past few years, he had been keeping her safe from Montoya and Ortiz, and now, she runs right back into the fire.

Once the plane landed, Nehemiah was met at the airport by a federal agent.

"Mr. Bolden. We have been expecting you. Please, follow me." The agent flashed his credentials too fast for Nehemiah, but he knew them to be the real thing.

"No." Nehemiah's statement halted the agent in his tracks.

"Excuse me. I apologize for giving you the impression you had a choice. Do not cause a scene. I am not alone. Please, follow me." The agent stood as tall as Nehemiah and had a menacing look to him. To people passing by, the two of them looked seconds from coming to blows. They stood toe to toe, and neither backed down. Nehemiah surveyed his surroundings and didn't see anyone who appeared out of place or to be watching them.

"Mr. Bolden, my men are better trained than you."

"I doubt that very seriously. Where are you taking me?" Nehemiah asked.

The agent did not respond, increasing Nehemiah's anger. Mac, nor Jake, had mentioned anything to him about the feds knowing he was arriving. This encounter felt like a set-up to him. He would go along with them for now, but he was keeping his eyes open.

There was an unmarked, black SUV waiting for them outside. Another agent was standing by the passenger door. Nehemiah, being observant, also spotted two additional SUV's parked further down the lane that led to the baggage claim area of the airport. Nehemiah smirked, they weren't nearly as good as they thought.

Observing every landmark on the hour-long drive was how Nehemiah was going to plan his escape if he had to. They stayed on the Expreso Cruz Ortiz Stella and passed Humacao. A few miles more, they were exiting onto Highway 906 and turning onto a secluded road.

The meeting point wasn't far from the toll road. He figured it was like hiding in plain sight since they turned off onto a dirt road between two residential areas. The two other black SUV's flanked them further up the road.

"Stay here," the agent instructed him.

Nehemiah had planned to do just that, until he saw Mac get out of one of the vehicles. What the hell was going on? Nothing was making sense to him anymore. The mission was to find Ortiz and Montoya, arrest them, and keep his family safe. Now, Nehemiah felt like he wasn't being told everything.

"Mr. Bolden, I thought I told you to stay in the vehicle."

"Well, I'm not good at following orders that are not given to me by my commanding officer, who happens to be standing right in front of me. Master Chief, what's going on?"

"We are taking you to a safe house. There is a bounty on your head for anyone who can bring you to Ortiz, dead or alive."

"I'd like to see them try."

"We figured you would say that. You don't have a choice in this matter."

Nehemiah was fuming with anger. There were still many unanswered questions. His priority right now was to find Gabriella and make sure she was safe. "What about my wife?"

"We know where she is. Don't worry about her. We need to keep you safe."

Everything that was happening was increasing his anger. How could Mac, of all people, tell him not to worry about his wife. Along with Jake and his brothers, Mac knew the most about his relationship with Gabriella and his daughters. Mac was the one who put the plan together to extricate them from Puerto Rico.

"So, you have eyes on her?" Nehemiah asked.

"She's fine. I won't let any harm come to her," Mac answered.

Ironically, those were the same words he said right before Chrystal was killed.

Nehemiah had nothing but time to think about his current situation. He was stuck in a federal safe house, surrounded by federal agents, and not knowing where Gabriella was. Not knowing if she was safe was driving him crazy. He was supposed to protect her and keep her safe, but like the others, he was failing at protecting.

He didn't protect his neighbor, he didn't protect Chrystal and now, he wasn't protecting Gabriella. This time was different than before; he didn't love those other women the way he loved Gabriella. Nehemiah had to figure out a way to get away from the safe house.

There were two agents in the house with him and two agents parked outside. Civic hadn't given him much information about the plan the feds had in place. Nehemiah figured that was because their priorities didn't line up. The government's priority was to catch Ortiz and stop his organization. Nehemiah's priority was to find his wife.

He walked over to the front window to try and locate the agents outside.

"Hey, step away from the window. It's for your security," the agent named Johnson told him.

"Why am I being secured? Why aren't we out there trying to find Ortiz?" Nehemiah was purposely trying to bait the agent into revealing something that could be useful for escape.

"Not my job. My orders are to stay here with you." Johnson returned his attention to the television. He was attentively watching a soccer game. The other agent's name was Moore, and he was reading a newspaper in the kitchen. Both were intentionally blocking the doors to exit the house.

For the time being, Nehemiah was stuck. He had no way out and no information. Gabriella was out there doing God knows what and he was unable to help. He took a seat on the sofa behind Agent Johnson and waited.

Chapter 11

Elijah drove the entire nine hours from Miami to Atlanta. The babies were being good, only waking to eat and have their diapers changed. Karyn was able to sleep most of the trip. Rachel ended up watching Disney movies with Jaleel; and when he went to sleep, she was able to pull out her tablet and finish up some work.

They arrived at the community of their rental house in the Tuxedo Park area of North Atlanta later than they originally told Neiko and Moses they would. Traffic was every bit of horrendous as people say it is. They were stuck on the expressway for over an hour, only moving about four miles in that time. Elijah was glad to see a gate and security. After giving the guard his name, they were allowed to pass through.

Hopefully, Ric or Moses would be at the house to give them the keys. Otherwise, they would all have to crash with Moses in his four-bedroom condo. Elijah didn't want to think of that; his brother's condo was on the other side of downtown, and that meant more traffic.

There were two cars in the drive way, neither appearing familiar to Elijah. He was cautious as he slowly approached the front of the house. The first vehicle had Georgia license plates, and the second vehicle had Michigan license plates. His nerves lessened, seeing as they had family and friends from both locations.

Elijah decided not to park next to the unknown vehicles. Instead, he parked a few cars' length in front of the first car on the circular driveway. His immediate concern was his family and being prepared if they needed a quick getaway. Being a celebrity kept him on high alert.

"You guys stay in the car. Rachel get in the driver's seat. Keep the car running. I have a strange feeling about this," Elijah said.

Elijah walked toward the house and noticed the door was open and voices were coming from inside.

"Hello, is someone here?" He asked, taking precaution as he entered.

"Of course, someone is here. What took you guys so long?" Monica asked walking to greet him in the front foyer. She was looking as beautiful as ever. Elijah had to make room for her pregnant belly as he hugged her and kissed her cheek. He, then, noticed movement behind them and saw Ric walk by on his cell phone.

"What are you two doing here?" Moses had told Elijah that someone from the rental company would be there to meet them with the keys.

"We got here first. Then we decided to stay and greet you the proper way. Where is Karyn and my babies?"

"They are still in the car. Your cars didn't look familiar to me at all. I was being cautious."

Monica gave him a side eye. They were in one of the most affluent areas of Atlanta, and he knew it. They had to pass several million-dollar homes to get to this one. She left him standing there as she walked outside to get her friend.

Ric was putting his phone away as he entered the great room. "Sorry about that. Work issues, nothing big. How was the trip?"

"Not bad at all. I thought it would be much worse with babies in the car, but they slept most of the time."

"That's good. Moses did a good job of finding you a rental. This is a gated community and a nice pad. I'm thinking of looking around this area for something."

"Really? You and Monica finally giving up on living between two states?"

"Yeah, it's time to settle down and stay still."

"I understand. When did you get the Mercedes?" Elijah was referring to one of the vehicles outside.

"Nah, that's Scott car. We're driving the Range Rover. And before you start, we got a great deal on it, and it's used. So, I didn't go overboard on the price."

Elijah was the financial wizard of the family. While most people believed the Boldens were wealthy because of Evolution's fame, it was really because Elijah knew how to invest and convince others to invest and be smart with their money.

"Okay, so Scott is here," Elijah realized.

"Yeah, he's out back testing your grill. We thought we would have dinner ready for you guys when you arrived."

The two men started toward the door as Karyn, Rachel, and Monica entered carrying the babies and a sleeping Jaleel. They helped the ladies take the kids to a guest room, and then, they returned to the SUV to get all their luggage.

"This is nice. Who picked this out, you or Moses?" Rachel asked.

"Actually, I did." Scott answered, coming into the kitchen from the patio. "I told Moses about it when he mentioned you guys were coming this way." He was carrying a tray of food into the kitchen and spoke as he walked past.

Elijah thought he was seeing things, but there was a spark of something between Rachel and Scott. He wasn't sure what it was, but he was going to find out. Elijah may be the youngest in the family, but he was still protective of his sisters.

*****

Rachel wasn't sure how she should feel seeing Scott again so soon after he left Miami. She thought, for sure, she wouldn't still have goosebumps every time she saw him. And, the intensity of his eyes was calling to her. She just couldn't make out what they were saying.

She was trying not to act nervous or give anything away around her brother and sister-in-law. The ever-perceptive Elijah would catch on to anything and run with it. Already, she could see in her brother's eyes he was starting to detect something.

Quickly, Rachel grabbed her bag from Elijah and asked Monica where the other bedrooms were. The women went on a quick tour of the house, leaving the men to finish preparing dinner. If she had to stand there a second longer, she, for sure, would have started crying or something equally stupid. There was no way she was going to let Scott see how his leaving affected her.

There were five bedrooms and six bathrooms in the house. Monica led the way entering each room and speaking as if she were the real estate agent. The house was tastefully decorated with simple, but elegant, furnishings. Each bedroom and had a connecting bathroom and matching color schemes. Rachel decided on the room decorated in sky blue and silver. This room was on the opposite side of the house from the master bedroom where she was sure Elijah and Karyn would stay.

The master bedroom suite was decorated in dark oak wood. The four-poster bed dominated the huge room. The master suite also had a sitting area with a fireplace. The bathroom was a relaxation haven, complete with a sunken tub with jets and a separate shower that was also a steam room. The closet was the size of Rachel's bedroom in Miami, and that was saying a lot.

After placing nanny cams all around the house, the ladies returned to the kitchen. The men were putting the final touches on dinner. It was time for Rachel to put on her acting skills. She would need to endure a few hours with Scott. Prayerfully, it wouldn't be too bad; she enjoyed his company most of the time, and he was easy to talk with about anything. She just needed to keep it together.

Ric was lighting the candles on the table, Scott was pouring wine for everyone except Monica and Karyn, and Elijah was assisting the women into their chairs. Of course, Rachel would have to be seated next to Scott.

"Let us begin with a word of prayer," Elijah started. "Heavenly Father, thank you for all of your many blessings, friends, and family. Thank you for your traveling mercy." A series of amen's were said around the table. Elijah continued, "Watch over our family that could not be with us this evening. Keep them safe. Bless the food we are about to share and bless the hands that prepared it. In Jesus' name. Amen."

Rachel piled everything that was prepared on her plate. Food was her side-boo, and everyone knew it.

"I can't seem to understand where all of that food goes after she eats it," Monica mentioned, after watching Rachel balance a third dinner roll on top of her food.

"I have asked her the same thing since I met her. She eats all day and never gains a pound," Karyn responded.

Rachel laughed and said, "I have a good metabolism and high energy that needs to be fed." She started right in on the beef BBQ ribs that Scott prepared. "Oh, my goodness, Scott, these ribs are amazing. The bone slid right off."

"Dang, Rachel, do you have to talk with your mouth full? You will never find a man doing that at the dinner table," Karyn joked with her.

Rachel immediately stiffened at her sister-in-law's words. She was afraid to look over at Scott for fear of giving something away.

Elijah was already suspicious, and she didn't want to give him any more ammunition.

She recovered quickly and said, "I don't need to worry about a man. Evolution Music is all I need."

"Still...don't you want a warm body to cuddle up to at night? Someone to tell your dreams and fears to?" Monica asked.

"Hey, my sister doesn't need a man to cuddle with. Stop giving her ideas," Elijah chimed in; spoken like a true big brother, even though he was younger by two years.

"Elijah, seriously? She is almost 30 years old. I'm not giving her ideas, I'm sure she has thought about it already." Monica said.

Rachel kept her head down, not making eye contact with anyone. She couldn't believe the topic of dinner was her love life or lack thereof. Instead of participating in the conversation, she continued stuffing her face.

After dinner, Rachel volunteered to clean up the kitchen. It was her way of saying thanks to her brother for letting her tag along. And, a way to get away from Scott's presence and try to clear her head. Unfortunately for Rachel, Scott stayed behind to help her while the others went out to sit by the pool.

"Rachel, listen. I'm sorry about the way I left things in Miami."

"What do you mean?" Rachel asked, nonchalantly. "It's not like we were in a relationship or anything." She rinsed a few dishes before placing them in the dishwasher. His presence around her was causing her emotions to go out of whack again. She wanted to hate him, but what he did was probably for the best. She was clearly more invested in the friendship than he was.

"I get it, but I could have been a little more considerate of your feelings. I apologize." Scott took a plate from her hands and placed it in the dishwasher. The two of them worked together silently cleaning the kitchen. After everything was taken care of, Scott gently tugged at Rachel's hands.

"How long are you planning to stay in Atlanta?" he asked.

"Not sure. Why?"

"Just curious, I guess. I'm about to head back to my apartment. Ric was kind enough to lease a corporate apartment for me. I'm starting to like this company security stuff."

"That's good. Well, have a nice evening." Rachel removed her hands from his and left him staring at her back. She was grateful that he didn't try to stop her from walking away.

Rachel went into the bedroom she would be using and closed the door behind her. Her thoughts and emotions were all over the place. She was almost thirty years old and still having childhood crushes on boys. Going through all this turmoil over a guy who was never hers to begin with, was why she stayed far away from men.

She had to get over this infatuation she had with Scott. He was Monica's brother for heaven's sake. He would be around family for years to come. She had to get her head back on straight and move forward. She was the CEO of a major record company, not some college nitwit with her first heartbreak.

"Pull it together chick," she said to herself.

Rachel opened her overnight bag and pulled out her Bible; the old King James Version Bible that used to sit on the table in her grandmother's house. It was worn, but still served its purpose. Every time Rachel read this Bible, she felt closer to her grandmother.

She opened the bible and instinctively turned to 1st Corinthians 16:14. *"Do everything in love."* She sighed heavily and turned a few pages and landed at Ephesians 4:2. *"Be completely humble and gentle; be patient, bearing with one another in love."*

That's it, she thought. She closed the bible and placed it back in her bag. God was not playing fair. Trying to convince herself it was not God, but just the luck of the page, she opened the bible, again, and flipped pages until it landed back on 1st Corinthians. This page was heavily outlined in yellow highlighter. Her grandmother must have really loved this passage. It read, *"And now these three remain: faith, hope, and love, but the greatest of these is love."*

Rachel gave up and accepted that God was talking to her through scripture. Have faith, be patient, have hope, and remember to love.

1 John 4:16: "And so we know and rely on the love God has for us. God is love. Whoever lives in love lives in God, and God in them."

Chapter 12

Scott had been working late hours for the past few days. Learning the ins and outs of not only building security, but also, cyber-security. As the new director, he felt he needed to know as much as possible, even if he didn't have the technical skill.

Most of the time, he was training on some new security system, but his mind would go back to Rachel. He could still see her face when he left Miami, and then, he remembered her trying to hold it together when they were alone in the kitchen the other night.

He shouldn't think about her so much, but there was a draw that kept pulling them together. He couldn't ignore it anymore. Scott had a plan of how he was going to get back into good standing with the boss lady. He was accepting his destiny and, like it or not, she was it.

Scott tried to refocus on the screen in front of him for the umpteenth time. Figuring that he wasn't going to get anywhere with the training, he started checking his emails. One caught his attention.

The cyber-security team was bringing a potential situation to his attention. Cyber-security also handled security clearances for all employees. During their background investigation, a sealed file kept appearing for one of their provisional, contract employees. Anthony Shaw had been working for Diaz, Inc. for just under a month. He was limited in his access to the company due to his lack of clearance.

Scott found it unusual that a low-level technician would have a sealed file. He called around to some old Navy buddies of his that were now working for the FBI. Even they were unable to open the file. Without knowing what was in the file, Scott was not about to approve Mr. Shaw's clearance.

"Hey, Neal, can you take a look at this?"

Neal Hamilton was the lead Information Systems Technician. He had been with Diaz for the last two years, after completing an extensive internship program. Ric had only wanted the best employees. He set up several internship programs in various departments. The internships were actual competitions for a job at Diaz, Inc.

"What am I looking for?" Neal asked.

"Tell me if you see anything out of the ordinary."

Neal took his time scouring the pages of intel about Anthony Shaw, and then, suddenly stopped. "This guy, Shaw...his file is sealed, but not by the FBI."

"Okay, who has sealed it?"

"That's a good question. Let me see something." Neal's finger went to work, punching keys faster than anyone Scott had ever seen. "Interesting," he said. His fingers started at rapid speed, again. Then, suddenly, Neal leaned back in his chair and placed his hands behind his head. "There you go. Man, my skill even amazes me."

"Get out of the way, kid genius. What am I looking at?" Scott asked.

"The file was sealed at a local level. They only stay sealed for 10 years. It's public record now; if you know what you are looking for."

"Good job, Neal. Now don't mention this to anyone. This is now a project only you and I are working on. We'll tell Ric when we get to the bottom of everything.

For the next few hours, the two men worked feverishly to uncover whatever it was that Anthony Shaw was hiding. Neal was able to tap into secured federal databases, and with some help from Scott's friends, they were able to find a connection that would be of interest to Ric and Nehemiah.

Anthony Shaw's real name was Antonio Montoya, brother to Carlos Montoya of San Juan, Puerto Rico. Scott immediately pulled out his cell phone and called Ric.

"It's 3 AM, what the hell do you want?" Ric answered.

"Sorry to wake you up bro, but you might want to get down here and see what we just uncovered."

"I'm on my way." Ric disconnected the call.

The three men sat around the computer in Scott's office and stared at the information – no one knowing what to say. Before Ric arrived, Neal was able to find some more information on Anthony Shaw. It appears he was arrested, but never charged with human trafficking over 10 years ago. Mr. Shaw turned over evidence and cooperated with the U.S. District Attorney to be able to walk away with no record and a sealed file.

"Have you been able to get Nehemiah on the phone?" Scott asked Ric.

"Calls keep going to voicemail. With everything that is going on with him and Gabriella, it's not like him to turn his phone off."

"Yeah. I haven't heard from him since the family conference call."

Scott felt something was off with Nehemiah. He decided to follow-up on his gut feeling by calling Elijah. Ric agreed that if anyone knew something, it would be Elijah. This type of thing couldn't wait until morning.

Elijah answered the phone a little livelier than Scott expected for someone to be at 5am.

"Sorry to wake you, man."

"Don't be. I was already awake. The twins like to eat every odd hour. What's going on?"

"I have you on speaker with Ric. We are in the office and discovered something. Have you heard from Nehemiah?"

"Not for a few weeks. Last I heard from my dad, he was headed to San Juan."

"San Juan?" Ric and Scott spoke at the same time.

"Yeah, something about Gabriella running away and going back to San Juan to finish what she started. She left the girls with my parents. Does what you found have anything to do with that?"

"We think so. Can you try to get in touch with him?"

"I can try but when he is working a mission, it is not likely he will surface until he is ready."

"Thanks, Elijah."

Chapter 13

Nehemiah had been trapped in this supposed safe house for two days. The agents rotated out every twelve hours, but never giving Nehemiah any real amount of time to be alone. He was getting cabin fever to the extreme because he was stuck here, and he had no idea where Gabriella was or if she was safe.

The only highlight of being trapped and caged like an animal was the meals. Each day, meals were delivered, and the food had been delicious. On this day, lunch had included mofongo, a popular Afro-Puerto Rican dish made with fried plantains and vegetables mashed with garlic, and fried pork.

It was almost time for a shift change. Nehemiah had been studying each of the agents, trying to uncover a weakness. Something he could manipulate so he could escape. Unfortunately, these guys were very well trained. Nehemiah was heading back to his room to be alone when Agent Moore's phone rang.

"Yeah. Okay." Moore put his phone away and said to Johnson, "Open the door. Civic is coming in."

Master Chief McEntire entered the house dressed in civilian attire, unlike he had when they last saw each other. He scanned the room before continuing all the way into the house and stopping in front of Nehemiah.

Nehemiah was beyond pissed with his commanding officer. He needed to be out in the field looking for Gabriella. Mac knew that, and of all people, he should understand.

"Master Chief," Nehemiah spoke first.

"Bolden, have a seat. We need to talk."

Nehemiah noticed that Moore and Johnson were both in the living room watching television. They were far enough away to be out of earshot of the conversation.

"Have you found my wife?"

"She wasn't lost. And, she is safe."

Nehemiah had not realized he was holding his breath until he heard she was safe.

"We are bringing you into the mission now. We needed to make sure that Gabriella hadn't defected."

"You know she is clean. Whatever is going on, she had to think this was the only way to end things."

"Well, we still don't know what she was thinking. Right now, neither Montoya, nor Ortiz, knows she is back. She has been staying with an older lady in Old San Juan. The lady leaves every morning and sets up her stand at the market, and then, goes home. We haven't put eyes on Gabriella yet, but we know she is there."

Nehemiah knew the older woman. The same woman from the market when he first met Gabriella. He had never asked Gabriella how she knew the woman, but thinking back now, the woman did seem to know a lot about Gabriella.

"Is the woman in any danger?" Nehemiah asked.

"No. She is the informant."

*****

Scott and Ric had been trying to reach Nehemiah for two days. They gave the information they had to Jeremiah Bolden. They were told he would know what to do with it. Scott decided that he didn't want to dwell on it any further, at least, not until Nehemiah got back to him. Until then, Mr. Shaw's security clearance would be on hold.

It was lunchtime and the rumble of his stomach reminded Scott that he had not eaten breakfast. He closed his laptop and made his way for the elevators. He hated to eat alone and thought about asking one of the guys in security if they wanted to go to the burger joint not far from the building. Scott decided against that, not wanting to seem as if he were showing any type of favoritism toward any employee. The retiring head of security always told him to keep it professional.

He remembered that Rachel had been using an empty office in the building. Scott pulled his phone from his pocket and called Rachel. She answered on the first ring.

"Rachel Bolden."

"Rachel Bolden, this is Scott Heller."

"Oh, Scott, I'm sorry, I didn't know it was you. The name showed private on my caller ID. Most of my clients keep their numbers private."

"No problem. I was calling to see if you would like to go to lunch with me?"

"I don't think so. I have a ton of work to do, and I am meeting with a realtor in a few hours."

"A realtor? Are you thinking of moving to Atlanta?"

"No. Elijah is thinking about it. I am thinking about adding a recording studio."

Scott had almost jumped to conclusions assuming that she was following him to Atlanta. He was glad she wasn't thinking about moving. Not because he didn't want her around, but because he was thinking of returning to Miami. Corporate security was cool, but a bit stagnant and dull most of the time. He had given

Nehemiah's offer more thought and figured he was very qualified to work for him.

"Oh, okay. Well, I promise to have you back within the hour. There is a Greasy Spoon not far from the building, and you would love the portion sizes."

"I'm not sure if that was a compliment or not."

"I just know that eating is one of your favorite things."

"Okay, I really do have a lot of work to do. I have to be back in an hour. I'll meet you downstairs in the lobby."

Scott was smiling when he got off the elevator and ran into Ric and Monica. His sister was six months pregnant and remained stylish in her long blue sundress. She rocked a pair of Chuck Taylor Converse's like none other. Monica had to be one of few women who would wear the classic basketball shoes with a formal gown or jeans.

"What are you smiling for, Big Brother?" Monica greeted him with a hug.

"It's a beautiful day, and I am on my way to lunch."

"With anyone we know?"

"Monica, stay out of the man's business," Ric told her, grabbing her around the waist before kissing her. "I thought you were so tired that you needed to rest before going home?"

"I am. Bye, Brother." Monica walked toward the elevators with her husband, then turned back to her brother when she saw Rachel coming toward them.

"Hi, Rachel. Bye, Rachel," she said.

Rachel smiled at the greeting, then frowned upon approaching Scott. "What was that all about?" she asked, pointing behind to where Monica and Ric disappeared onto the elevator.

Scott wanted to strangle his sister, but he loved her so much. Instead of being mad at Monica, he gently grasped Rachels' hand and led her toward the front entrance. "That was nothing. My sister is baby delirious, that's all."

The Greasy Spoon was just like the one in Miami. A small eatery with a lot of attitude. The smells of different types of foods mingling together would cause some to turn their noses up, but for a true foodie like Rachel, she seemed excited.

They found a booth near the back of the restaurant, out of the line of sight of the front door. The booth afforded some privacy and Scott needed to talk to her.

She was young and beautiful, and he wasn't sure what he wanted at the moment. Having the military as his entire life for 20 years, he was having difficulty adjusting to civilian life, but every time he saw Rachel, and looked into her eyes, he could see a future with her. And, that's what scared him the most.

Scott watched the way Rachel's eyes got bigger as she read the menu. He enjoyed watching her in her happy place.

"What are you having?" he asked her.

"Everything looks so good, but I think I am going for the shrimp and grits. With a side salad and a huge slice of caramel cake. What are you getting?"

Scott was unable to contain his laughter. "It is truly a marvel how you are able to eat so much and look as beautiful as you do every day."

"Scott, you shouldn't say things like that," she blushed, shyly lowering her head.

"So, the boss lady blushes. Looks good on you. I like it."

Before Rachel could say anything in response, the waiter approached to take their order.

"I will have the catfish dinner with collard greens and candied yams as my sides. The lady will have a side salad with vinaigrette dressing, an order of shrimp and grits, and a slice of the caramel cake. Make the cake to-go. And, gives us two glasses of water, both with lemon."

"You got it," the waiter said. Then, he took their menus and walked away.

"You remembered I like vinaigrette dressing on my salad," Rachel stated.

"I remember everything about you. And, there lies my problem." He grabbed both of her hands across the table. "I like you a lot, Rachel. Probably more than I should, but you deserve more than I can offer you. You are a music mogul working for your family's dynasty, and I barely have a job."

"That material stuff doesn't matter to me. You have been around my family enough times to know, the money and the fame doesn't mean anything to us. It's work to us. Hard work; and that is all we care about."

Scott thought about her statement for a few seconds. The Bolden family was probably the most down to earth family he had ever met. They had their share of dramas and issues, but love kept them grounded. Love for each other, and love for Christ. That fact was evident in everything they did. He had never seen a family pray as much as they do.

"Rachel, I want to get to know you better, but only if you understand, I am still working through some things. So, let's be friends, hang out, have fun and see what happens."

The first look she had, was perplexing, then, she smiled. Scott released a breath he didn't know he was holding. At least she wasn't crying or yelling. He hoped that the smile meant she was on board with his idea of being friends.

"I can do friends," she said.

Scott relaxed. He hadn't realized he had been tensely awaiting her response. He smiled and said, "You know what this means? This means you and I will have to spend time with one another and have fun. I already know there will be lots of eating in the future. Seeing as I can't eat like you, we will need to partake in lots of outdoor physical activity. We should start by going walking tonight."

"Walking?"

"Yeah, we can get in our required number of steps at Six Flags." Scott knew that would get a smile out of her. He loved to see her smile, and he was determined that while they were friends, he would keep her smiling. That's what friends were for.

*****

"What are you thinking about?" Karyn asked her husband, who appeared to be deep in thought, staring out into space. He was sitting in a lounge chair on the patio that led to the swimming pool area.

He turned upon hearing her voice and held out his hand to her. She easily accepted it and welcomed the embrace she knew was coming. Elijah was a very affectionate husband. He loved hugging and touching his wife. He never shied away from public displays of affection.

Pulling Karyn in front of him and hugging her tightly, he said, "I was thinking about Rachel. Do you think she works too much?"

"So, you noticed too?"

"Noticed what?" he asked.

"Don't play stupid with me. You noticed the looks and sparks of desire between her and Scott."

"Stop, please. Don't say desire with regards to my sister," he joked. "Seriously, I noticed, but what I also realized is she has never been in a romantic relationship. She came to work for me right after college."

"What makes you think she didn't have a boyfriend in college?"

"Rachel was only about books. If she did have a boyfriend, he didn't last long. When she came to work for me, she never looked back."

Rachel had attended college in California, far away from her parents. She needed to be independent, and her parents didn't argue with her. They let her go across the country for four years but made sure she knew her family loved her and would always be there for her.

When she returned home after graduation, she immediately asked Elijah for a job. She moved to Miami where Evolution Music was based and quickly climbed the corporate ladder of her on accord, and not because she was the boss' sister. She was responsible for opening the recording studio as another stream of income, and she, alone, revamped the talent acquisition department.

Rachel rightfully earned her title of CEO of Evolution Music when Elijah stepped down after getting married. She was driven and successful, but Elijah wondered if she was happy.

"I like Scott," Elijah said. "He seems like a great guy. I hope he doesn't hurt her."

"He isn't like that. I think we need to sit back and just watch what happens. You may be surprised." Karyn turned in her husband's arms and gave him a sultry look.

"Karyn, stop it. It hasn't been six weeks. You know what the doctor said."

She frowned at him and tried to pout. When that didn't work, she whispered a love thought in his ear. That had Elijah lifting her in his arms and walking back into the house. Before they could make it to the bedroom, the cell phone in his back pocket started ringing.

Elijah growled into his phone, "This had better be good."

"The best, man. Neiko is in labor. We're at the hospital now."

Placing his wife gently on the floor, he whispered to her, "Neiko is in labor," before speaking back to his brother. "Alright, Moses. We're on our way."

Karyn was already headed to the bedroom to get dressed and to get the babies and Jaleel ready to go meet their new cousin. Another Bolden grandchild was about to be born.

Six hours later, Moses Nicolas Bolden II was born.

Chapter 14

Nehemiah was brought up to speed on the investigation. Gabriella was still in danger until Montoya and Ortiz were completely out of the picture. What scared him most were the thoughts he was having killing the two men and anyone associated with them. He wanted his family to live without fear.

An agent had been embedded within the Ortiz organization for the past year. There was rendezvous happening at Club Inferno. There was no way Nehemiah could go in with the bounty on his head. The plan was for him to run communication from the command center they had set-up a few miles from the club.

The informant had passed intelligence that Montoya would be at the club to meet with Gabriella. She would be surrounded by agents and would be in no danger. As soon as contact was made, the agents would be there to take Montoya into custody.

"What about Ortiz?" Nehemiah asked.

"It's unlikely that Ortiz will be at the club. He has been underground for years and only communicates through his people.

Nehemiah didn't like this plan. There were too many unknown factors, and none of them ended with Ortiz in handcuffs or dead. Those were the only two available outcomes Nehemiah wanted.

"So, you want me to stay in a van a few miles from the club, while my wife meets with the man who used to beat the crap out of her? The same man who forced her to traffic young girls overseas?" Nehemiah had the look of murder in his piercing dark eyes. Civic even took a step back from fear of what Nehemiah might do.

"You will stay in the van. You are not retired yet, Angel." Using his mission code name was an indication that he was to follow orders, but there was more to this than Civic was letting on. Nehemiah would stand down until all was revealed.

"When does this mission happen?"

"In about six hours. Agent Johnson will bring you to the command center." Civic patted Nehemiah on the back before leaving the room. He then, turned back and said, "Angel, remember, observation not engagement."

Nehemiah realized it wasn't what Civic said, but how he said it. He also noticed the hand signal that he gave as he walked from the room and out of the house. Their team had created their own method of communication to include code words, hand signals, and even bird calls.

The signal Civic had just given to Nehemiah told him to watch out for other clues during this mission. The other agents probably had no idea of what was about to happen. He would just bide his time until the mission began.

A few hours later, Nehemiah was in a utility van with Agent Johnson, parked about three blocks from the warehouse that housed Club Inferno. He remembered the area from years ago when had been there.

They had approximately five agents on the inside; two females and three males. One of the female agents had been a bartender at Inferno for the past six months. She was the one who would make the signal that Montoya or Ortiz was in the club.

Nehemiah's job was just to survey the area. Watch the cars that passed on the way toward the warehouse and watch the two live streams coming from body cams being worn by the agents inside. He prayed this would be the end to Ortiz and Montoya. It was time he and Gabriella could have a normal family and lifestyle.

Several cars had passed in the past hour and nothing seemed out of place.

"This seems like a bust. Nothing happening out here," Johnson said.

"The night is still early. How many of these have you done?" Nehemiah asked.

"A few. I'm experienced, if that's what you're asking," Johnson answered, with slight annoyance to his voice.

That was exactly what Nehemiah had been doing. Trying to determine if he could dupe the agent. Trying to find ways out of the van was proving to be difficult.

Agent Johnson was right, the evening turned out to be a bust. Not only didn't Ortiz or Montoya show up, but no one associated with them even came near the club. Nehemiah was beginning to think they received bad intel.

Everyone arrived back to the safe house a few hours later. They were waiting for Civic and the agent-in-charge to return. Things were about to get really ugly. Either, the intel was bad, or there was a leak in the team. If there was a leak, that meant Gabriella could potentially be at risk.

Civic entered the house, making contact, first, with Nehemiah and then, with the other agents. Then, the agent-in-charge entered, and immediately started cursing. He demanded answers, and no one was speaking up. Nehemiah watched the other men and tried not to laugh. The agent-in-charge saw his smile.

"Do you find something funny, Petty Officer Bolden?"

"No, Sir. I'm just happy that I have been under watch and didn't have anything to do with it." Before the agent could start with his curse-laden tirade again, Nehemiah spoke, again. "But it makes me wonder if Gabriella Bolden is in any danger."

The agent became enraged again and jumped in Nehemiah's face. "Don't think it's lost on me that your wife is the reason we are even in this position!" he shouted.

Nehemiah stood toe to toe with the agent. "I don't care what you think! My wife's safety is my priority and taking down Ortiz and Montoya ensures she remains safe for the rest of her life. It seems we are on the same page," he said, through clenched teeth.

Civic stepped in to try to diffuse the situation. "Stand down, Angel." When he noticed Nehemiah refused to move, he repeated himself more forcefully this time. "I said, stand down."

This time, Nehemiah took a step back, never taking his eyes from the agent.

"We are back at square one and now I am taking over this mission," Civic announced.

That statement got the agent to finally look away from Nehemiah. "What do you mean you are taking over? I am the agent-in-charge."

"You *were* in charge. As of five minutes ago, you have been relieved. When my team takes over, we get results. There is a problem in your team that you need to work on. In the meantime, you and your team are dismissed. My team will be here by the morning.

The agent-in-charge was fuming but didn't fight what he was being told. He had received a message that told him to pack it up. Agent Johnson and Moore bid their farewells and left along with everyone else.

Once everyone, except Nehemiah and Civic, had gone, there was a knock at the door. Jake, who now had a code name of, Flip, because Civic was able to flip him back to government employment, entered, followed by Pac-Man and Zeus. The men greeted each other and immediately began to devise a new plan. Nehemiah was more confident, now, with his team in place.

The new plan was to use Nehemiah as bait. Montoya had a personal vendetta against him. And, if the chatter was any good, Ortiz wanted him dead, as well. While they waited to implement their new plan, the team received new intel that Gabriella was still with the informant and safe. Ortiz had just arrived on the island and was looking for Nehemiah. He had placed a bounty of $100,000 for Nehemiah, dead or alive.

*****

Ric and Scott were in the security office of the Diaz building looking over some more information they found on Mr. Shaw. They had been patiently waiting to hear from Nehemiah. For two weeks, they had been sitting on the security clearance for Mr. Shaw. They had granted him a provisional and told him it was standard procedure to do so.

He seemed to accept Scott's explanation of why he wasn't being allowed into certain areas or access to certain files. The delay would only hold for so long before Mr. Shaw became suspicious.

Ric was about to leave the security office when his cell phone rang, and he saw it was Nehemiah. He signaled for Scott to join him in the adjoining conference room. The room was typically used for training new security personnel.

"This is, Ric. Man, it's good to hear from you."

"Sorry about that. I was being detained. I got word from my dad that you have information."

"Yeah, Scott found something interesting about one of our contractors. I'll let Scott tell you." Ric placed the call on speaker and Scott informed Nehemiah of everything he found on Mr. Shaw.

"You have got to be kidding me. That is what we have been looking for. The missing piece."

"How so?" Scott asked.

"Mr. Shaw is going to be our way in."

The next day, Anthony Shaw was met at the front door of the Diaz building by two federal agents, Scott, and Ric. They escorted him to one of the first-floor conference rooms.

"What is this all about?" Mr. Shaw asked.

No one answered him. They all stood around him without saying a word. The phone in the center of the table rang and Ric reached for it. "This is Ric."

"We're ready," Nehemiah replied.

Ric went to the laptop at the end of the table and pulled up a video feed on the screen behind him. Instantly, Nehemiah's face appeared.

"Mr. Shaw. Or, should I say, Antonio Montoya. I am a federal agent along with the other two men who brought you in today."

"What is the meaning of this?" Anthony asked, defensively.

"Mr. Montoya…" Ric continued.

"My name is Shaw."

Nehemiah ignored his declaration and continued, "Mr. Montoya, your brother is Carlos Montoya, and he is wanted on a federal arrest warrant for drug and child trafficking, but you know this don't you?" When Shaw remained quiet, Nehemiah continued. "We know all about the agreement you have in place. We are not going to compromise that deal, but we are seeking your assistance with apprehending your brother. It seems you conveniently forgot to mention him when you were working with the Drug Enforcement Agency. We will not inform the DEA of your omission, if you help us catch Carlos."

The room remained silent for a few minutes. Shaw looked around the room, seeming to weigh his options. He, then, agreed to whatever they needed.

Overnight, Nehemiah discovered that the brothers were not as close as he was with his family. The Montoya brothers grew up not knowing they were related at all. Their first meeting was at their mother's funeral. Carlos was raised by his maternal grandmother, and Antonio was brought up in the foster care system, not knowing his parentage until he was an adult.

After bouncing around from foster homes to juvenile detention centers, Antonio got connected with the underworld of illegal gambling and drugs. Unbeknownst to him, his brother was mixed up in a similar world. Antonio eventually got caught and was offered a deal from the DEA. His deal included a change of name and relocation stateside.

"Ric, Scott, thanks for everything," Nehemiah said, after they had devised a plan with Antonio's assistance.

"No problem, man. Be safe out there," Scott replied.

"We're praying for you," Ric added.

Scott turned to Ric and deeply exhaled. "You know, when I retired from the military, I thought this part of my life was over. I thought I would be on a beach somewhere with margaritas and babes."

"But now, you kind of miss the fast pace of investigations?"

"Actually, no. I miss being a part of a team. Being a part of something that is bigger than me. Is that crazy?"

"No, it's not. You just need to find a new team. The Diaz team would love for you to stay, but I have a feeling this isn't really what you were looking for, either. Before you decide, pray about it first."

Scott realized Ric was able to effectively read him and was grateful for his understanding. He was truly happy his sister found a man like Ric.

A few hours later, Scott was waiting for Rachel in the lobby. They had gone to lunch every day since their impromptu visit to Six Flags. Rachel admitted that was the most fun she had ever had. Scott had to also admit, he had not enjoyed a date like that in a long time.

He stopped himself at the thought of it being a date. Was it really a date to him? He wondered if Rachel thought it was a date.

Chapter 15

Nehemiah had been in the safe house with Pac-Man for two days. He never noticed it before, but Pac-Man could put away two entire pizzas alone and remained in tip-top shape. The guy couldn't have an ounce of fat on him. Zeus and Flip were staying in San Juan keeping an eye on things. Civic kept everyone informed from an undercover position at Roosevelt Roads.

Tomorrow night, they would be returning to Inferno. Apparently, the leak did not come from the undercover agents that worked there. The bartender was now feeding information to Civic directly.

Pac-Man was in a food coma; his huge frame laid across the sofa in the main living area. Nehemiah was trying to take a nap, as well. The mission would be risky, and they needed to be well rested and on high alert.

The dream always started at the same place...with Nehemiah crotched down in a closet, armed with a sniper rifle, preparing to take out the enemy. The room was filling with smoke, but not a toxic gas. They were trying to make it difficult to see inside. The hostiles were holding sixteen hostages. No one was moving, and he didn't know if they were dead or alive.

Five terrorist hostiles had taken over a ballroom in the resort. Mostly tourists were staying there. Civic had gotten into place on the other side of the ballroom through a vent. Pac-Man was securing the perimeter of the building. They had to be sure it was just these five hostiles. The three of them were preparing to breach when she entered the room.

"Angel, keep your eyes open. The informant said we'd know him when we see him."

"Copy that, Civic." Nehemiah kept his rifle trained on the leader.

"Angel, come in."

"Go, Civic."

"We have a friendly to your 9 o'clock."

"Where? I don't see anyone?" Nehemiah whispered. Then, he heard her voice.

"Do you have my money?" she asked the leader of the group.

Nehemiah was confused. What was she doing there? How did she get into the ballroom with the hostages? One of the gunmen walked over to the leader and uttered something to him. The leader took a step back and held his gun up to her head.

"You thought you could trick me. Stupid American." He pulled the trigger.

Using her military training, she was able to dodge the shot and sweep the leg of the gunman, causing him to fall backward. Nehemiah didn't wait for the command to breach. Instead, he jumped out of the closet and shot one hostile between the eyes. Chrystal had taken out another hostile leaving two against two.

Nehemiah didn't see Civic anywhere. He had to have seen him rush into the room.

"Put your weapon down!" Nehemiah yelled.

The four of them had guns trained on each other. If only Civic would come out now, they could end this.

"Put your weapon down, before you become an angel." Chrystal said.

"Silver, what are you doing?" Nehemiah asked, without lowering his rifle.

"What does it look like? I'm taking care of business." She, then, aimed her gun at Nehemiah, and a shot rang out.

There was a hard knock to the door. Nehemiah sprang from the chair he was uncomfortably sitting in. Pac-Man jumped up at the same time. Both immediately reached for their firearms, without saying a word.

"Señor, you asked for towels," the voice on the other end said.

He knew her voice, but also remembered that was what she said to him the day their lives changed. It was Gabriella at the door; but how? Nehemiah took precaution by looking out of the window first, before opening the door and quickly snatching Gabriella inside. Without words, he held her tightly, not wanting to let her go.

"How did you get here?" he finally asked, while checking her over from head to toe.

"The old lady from the market told me you were here," she responded, attempting to hold in her tears. It was a failed attempt, and Nehemiah, again, held her tightly.

Pac-Man had gone out the back door to check the house and make sure she wasn't followed. He returned through the back door. "It's clear."

Nehemiah moved Gabriella into the kitchen and sat her at the table. Pac-Man grabbed an electronic device and used it to wave in front and behind her. They had to be sure she wasn't compromised or carrying any tracking devices.

She seemed to appear out of nowhere, and that caused the men to have plenty of questions.

"How did you get here? I didn't see a car outside," Pac-man started the questioning.

"I caught an Uber to a house two blocks away, and then I walked over here. I made sure to look for anything suspicious. I was not followed."

"Gabriella, you are not trained for this. You can't be sure no one followed you." Pac-man was angry and started rubbing his hand over his bald head. Nehemiah knew this pattern; he was thinking of every possible scenario.

Nehemiah finally found his voice and asked, "Why did you come here?"

"To warn you. Ortiz knows about the attempt to ambush him at Inferno. He has a spy on the inside. They know everything," she cried. When neither of the men spoke, she started again. "Nehemiah, I didn't want to leave. I swear, I didn't want to leave, but I had to. I can put a stop to all of this."

"How?" both men asked.

Before she could speak, the men's communication devices were alerting them that there was a message. Civic was on his way to the house. They had a bad feeling about what was about to happen next. They also weren't sure if they should hide Gabriella or not. Before Civic opened the door, they placed Gabriella in a back room. They'd keep her there until they determined it was safe for her to come out.

"Civic, what's up?" Nehemiah asked, trying to stay cool.

"Gabriella is missing. She was able to get some intel for us that she passed to the informant before leaving. I'm sorry, Angel, but I don't know where she is."

Pac-man re-directed Civic's attention to him, "What is the intel?"

"She was able to find out that Ortiz is having a meeting and not at Inferno. There is a mole on the inside of the DEA."

Nehemiah and Pac-Man exchanged glances and silently communicated that they should come clean. "Civic, Gabriella is here."

First, Civic's eye flinched and his jaw tightened. Then he gave both men the look that your dad would give when he wanted to be mad, but really couldn't. Instead of being angry, he was grateful that Gabriella had not been taken by Ortiz or Montoya. She was the wife of a team member, and she was safe. That was all Civic wanted.

They spent the next few hours reviewing the information that Gabriella brought to them. She had kept additional information in a safe deposit box to go along with the files from her flash drive. They had also received new intelligence from Flip and Zeus. With all of that, and the information they obtained from Antonio, Zeus was able to get close enough to Montoya to place a tracking device on him.

Zeus then tracked Montoya to the new rendezvous spot, which was corroborated by the bartender at Inferno. Before morning's dawn, Ortiz and Montoya would be in federal custody, and Nehemiah and Gabriella would be able to return home.

Later that evening, Civic arrived with Zeus and Flip to prepare for the mission. Since Flip was new to the team, he was assigned to run communications from the command center that would be stationed within a mile of the drop off site. Nehemiah hated leaving Gabriella alone for any length of time, but he had to finish this.

Nehemiah had not taken his eyes off of her since she arrived at the safe house, and he had no intention of leaving her alone again, until this mission began. The long stretches of time away from her and his family was over. He didn't care if he was officially retired or not. He would take her to work with him every day until his paperwork was signed. This ordeal had him seeing everything and everyone in a different light.

He and Gabriella had talked to their girls a few hours prior to let them know that mommy and daddy were okay. He didn't want them to worry. Jaclyn told the girls that they were on vacation and would be back real soon. When Nehemiah talked to his mother, he could hear the fear in her voice. That didn't stop her from telling him and Gabriella that they were loved.

Before Jaclyn would let them off the phone, she prayed for them. Until that moment, he never realized how much he appreciated her praying for him. His mother's prayers were expected, but this time, it was different. He truly felt God's presence, and a calm washed over him. Nehemiah was ready to accept God's will, whatever it may be.

The team was in position at the rendezvous point. Flip and Gabriella were about a mile away, inside of an old café that had been boarded up. He had a laptop set up on a dusty table and was connecting all of the team members to one of their individual communication devices. Then, he called out to each of them.

"Zeus?"

"Roger."

"Pac-Man?"

"Roger."

"Angel? Civic?

"Roger," they both responded.

The plan was to wait for Montoya and Ortiz to arrive, then take them without any casualties. The agent from Inferno had contacted Civic, letting him know that Ortiz was on his way, with a 10-minute ETA.

Everything was set-up and should happen just as planned. After 20 minutes and no one had arrived, Nehemiah got worried.

"Pac-Man, anything on your end?" Nehemiah asked.

"All quiet. That's not good."

Civic chimed in. "Zeus, what location do you have for Montoya?"

"His ping just stopped outside of the perimeter. Wait, it's starting to go backwards."

Nehemiah had a gut feeling something wasn't right. There is no way the intel wasn't good, unless…

"Civic, you thinking what I'm thinking?" Nehemiah asked.

"Flip? Come in Flip," Civic asked into the device.

There was no answer. Nehemiah left his post and took off at a sprint toward the command center. If Flip wasn't answering, they had to be in danger. Running, it would take Nehemiah 9 minutes to get to them. He prayed the entire way that he would get there in time.

Civic jumped in his truck and picked up Zeus on the way back to the center. Pac-Man was also a runner and caught up with Nehemiah just as he was about to storm the building. They quietly entered through a side door and encountered smoke. Nehemiah placed a finger over his lips and listened for voices or sounds of any kind.

The smoke was making it difficult for the men to see anything, but they both made it from the kitchen where they entered the main room to where Flip had set-up his equipment. The scene was all too familiar to Nehemiah. He started having momentary flashes of Chrystal. He had to find Gabriella, she had to be there.

"Well, well…it seems as the same cavalry that arrived last time is here to try to take me out, again," Ortiz said.

Nehemiah turned around quickly, with his gun aimed right for Ortiz. He would have taken the shot if Ortiz had not been holding Gabriella by the throat. Without lowering his weapon, Nehemiah spoke in a lethal low tone of voice. "Let her go."

"Why would I do that? She is the reason I lost my business five years ago. I told Carlos to handle his wife, but he didn't listen. Well, I took care of him, too. No honor amongst thieves."

The smoke was clearing, and Nehemiah could see Pac-Man moving behind Ortiz. In his peripheral vision, he also saw Civic coming in from the kitchen area. They had Ortiz surrounded. Now, to get Gabriella free of his grip.

"You don't really want her; you want me. I'm the one who took down your operation. I'm the reason you lost money."

"Nah, you're small fries, but Gabriella, she knows everything of the operation. She helped set up the organization, didn't you?" he pulled her closer.

Gabriella wasn't moving or saying anything. Ortiz was jerking her around like a rag doll, and each time he did so, Nehemiah flinched like he could feel her pain. He was watching the life drain from her body, and he was just standing there. She wouldn't have the same fate as Chrystal. He had to do something, quick.

Without a second thought, he knew he needed to get him to let her go. Instead of waiting for a signal from his team, Nehemiah charged Ortiz. The last thing he remembered was hearing the gunfire, and then, the acrid smell of gunpowder.

Chapter 16

Gabriella fell to the floor, grabbing for her throat, and gasping for air the minute Ortiz released her. Then, she remembered that he let her go because he had shot Nehemiah. She tried to come to her feet but was having a hard time breathing. Large arms grabbed her around the waist and pulled her from the floor and away from her husband. She struggled and tried to get free. She needed to get to Nehemiah.

"Gabriella, please come with me," she heard a voice say.

"No! No! No! I will not leave him." She was trying to fight back, but her entire body felt heavy, and everything was going dark. She felt her movements going in slow motion and voices were fading into the background.

"We are taking you to the hospital. You need to get checked, and then, you can be with him."

That was the last thing she heard before she passed out.

Gabriella was trying to open her eyes but found the task too difficult. She heard buzzers and beeps, noises and people, but didn't know where she was. There was so much movement around her. Like a flood, the memories started coming back to her. Ortiz had found her. She saw him before Flip did, but it was too late to scream; he had knocked Flip unconscious and grabbed her.

Then, Carlos walked into the room, smiling, like he knew some secret no one else knew.

"You thought you could run away from me? You are my wife. You will always be my wife. I don't care about any divorce papers."

"I told you to take care of her. You didn't. Now, I have to take care of you," Ortiz shouted.

Gabriella watched the smile from Carlos' face quickly change from smug to fear in a matter of seconds. Ortiz pointed the gun at him and said to Gabriella, "You are both liabilities. He was stupid, and so are you."

Just that quickly, Carlos was gone. In that moment, Gabriella knew she was going to die. She would never see her daughters or Nehemiah, again. No one was to blame, but herself. She got herself into this mess, and it only seemed right that she would pay with her life.

Ortiz grabbed Gabriella by the throat and severely hindered her airway. She tried to control her breathing, to buy her some time in hopes that Nehemiah or someone from the team would come to save her. That's when she heard someone enter the rear of the building. Ortiz heard it, too. He released his hold on her neck and told her to keep quiet or die. He, then, ignited two smoke bombs in the room and pulled her back into a corner and out of sight.

There was no sound, but she knew Nehemiah had come for her. She felt his presence and knew she had to hold on to life. The smoke was clearing, and Ortiz pulled her forward so Nehemiah could see them. Gabriella closed her eyes; she didn't want the fear in her husband's eyes to be the last thing she saw when she died.

They were talking, but she couldn't hear them any longer. Ortiz had increased the pressure around her neck, and she wasn't able to breathe. She could slowly feel herself fading away. Then, suddenly, she was falling. Before she hit the ground, she heard a gunshot, and then, seconds later, she felt arms wrap around her and pull her upwards from the floor.

She had been given oxygen in the ambulance and was taken to the Veterans Hospital in San Juan, along with her husband. The doctors had looked her over, and she was released with no significant injuries. Flip was found on the floor unconscious after a blow to the head; he was now in the emergency room being observed for having a concussion. Carlos was found dead, along with Ortiz. That was all she was able to gather from the doctors and nurses around her.

When Nehemiah charged at Ortiz, he released his grip on Gabriella, allowing Pac-Man a chance to shoot him three times to the chest. It was Zeus who gathered her from the floor, and Civic who told her that everything would be okay.

Now, she waited in the hospital for someone to give her an update on Nehemiah's condition. She hadn't seen his team members since they brought her into the hospital. She really needed someone to lean on right now…anyone. She hated waiting there alone.

Gabriella remembered something Jaclyn had told her during the time she stayed with the elder Boldens. *"If you truly trust God, pray and tell Him what you want. Tell Him what you need. He hears our prayers, and He is in the business of answering those prayers."*

She got to her knees and cried; but through her tears, she told God what she needed and what she wanted. She needed her husband to survive. Their children needed both of their parents. As she pleaded with God, she felt an immediate sense of calming that overtook her body. She heard whispers of God's voice telling her He was her comforter and that she was not alone.

She believed.

Gabriella drifted off to sleep on a lounge chair in the waiting room of the Intensive Care Unit. Nehemiah was still in surgery, but the nurses told her the better chairs and couches were in the ICU waiting room. She thought she was hearing things. In the recess of her mind, she could hear Tiffany's little voice calling to her. The sound started getting louder, and Gabriella struggled to open her eyes; but when she did, her daughter was standing right in front of her.

Gabriella jumped up too fast, causing her to become dizzy and nearly fall over. She, then, felt the embrace of someone. When she looked up, she saw her brother-in-law, Elijah. Her tears wouldn't stop flowing. She had prayed that his family was there with her. She had prayed that she wasn't alone in this waiting game.

"How did you know?" she asked through her tears.

"Mac called us, and we chartered a flight here," Elijah responded.

Thoroughly confused, she didn't understand how he got there so fast. Then, she realized he had said "*we.*" She looked around and all of Nehemiah's siblings were there, with their parents.

Tierra was asleep in the arms of her grandfather. Tiffany tightly hugged Gabriella's legs. She never wanted to let her go. Her tears wouldn't stop flowing, the love and concern from the Boldens were tremendous, and none of them had blamed her. She had never met a family like them in all her years.

"I knew the first faces Nehemiah wanted to see when he awakened would be his girls. All of his girls," Jaclyn told her.

For the next few hours, the family sat in the waiting room, each comforting Gabriella. She met Ruth, Aaron, and Moses for the first time. Just like Naomi and Elijah, they were just as nice and accepting of her.

The quietness of the room was interrupted when the doctor that had attended to Gabriella earlier came into the room. "Mrs. Bolden?"

Jaclyn and Gabriella both spoke, realizing the confusion, the doctor said again, "Mrs. Nehemiah Bolden?"

"Yes?" Gabriella answered.

"Your husband is out of surgery. He was very lucky. Two of the bullets hit him in the bullet-proof vest, one bullet hit him above the vest in the neck. That bullet was lodged close to the spinal cord. We were able to get all of the fragments out."

The doctor was hesitant, and Gabriella knew there was something he was not saying. "Doctor, please, just tell us," she pleaded.

"It was pretty touch and go in the operating room. It took us a while to control the bleeding. There was a lot of damage. We'll know more after the swelling goes down. He is one lucky young man."

"He's not lucky, he's loved," she said, as she looked around the room. "When can we see him?"

"Well, we don't want to overwhelm him. No more than two people at a time in the room. He is still on the ventilator, so don't expect him to be responsive. We are monitoring him closely."

"We understand, Doctor," Elijah told him. He, then, turned to Gabriella. "Let's pray before you go in to see him."

The entire family huddled together, holding hands, and built a circle around Gabriella. God had surely answered her prayers.

Gabriella had been sitting in the room with Nehemiah holding his hand for over an hour. The family wanted to give her time alone with him. She was forever grateful to her new family. They seemed to understand things before she could comprehend them.

"Gabriella? Do you want anything to eat or drink?" Rachel asked her.

"No," she responded, not looking away from Nehemiah.

"Mom said Tierra didn't need to see him like this. Dad went to the hotel to get everyone checked in for the night. She allowed Tiffany to stay. I hope that was okay."

"Yes, that's fine."

Rachel moved to sit in a chair on the opposite of the bed as Gabriella. "You know, when I was little, I always knew Nehemiah would be the son to follow in our father's footsteps. In his teenage years, he changed. One day, he was this popular star swimmer in high school, and the next, he was always serious and almost dangerous, but he always, and I mean always, looked out for the women in his family and any female he thought needed help. He would intimidate bullies in school if they were messing with a girl. He just had that protective instinct."

Gabriella hadn't acknowledged Rachel was talking. She was talking, not just for Gabriella, but also, for herself.

"He was always the hero. It's hard seeing him as a mere mortal." She started crying. "I'm going to send my mother in now."

Jaclyn entered the room holding Tiffany's hand. Gabriella released Nehemiah's hand for the first time since being in the room with him and reached for her daughter.

"Grandma told me what to expect. I'm not afraid." She touched her father's hand, where her mother's had just been. "Dad, it's Tiffany. If you can hear me, listen, okay? Mom is crying, and you remember saying that you hate to see her cry? When you wake up, she won't cry anymore, okay? Grandma said the same thing you always tell me. Even though things don't seem okay doesn't mean that God isn't working in the background on your behalf. I know He is working in the background. I love you, Dad." Tiffany kissed her mother's cheek and left the room.

"That girl is wise way beyond her years. You have done such a good job raising her," Jaclyn said, taking the seat Rachel vacated earlier.

"Tiffany has always been that way. She has really blossomed since Nehemiah has been in her life," Gabriella replied, still not looking away from her husband.

"Even though she is not his biological daughter, they are so much alike," Jaclyn said. She grabbed his other hand and held it, rubbing her thumb over the back of his hand.

They remained silent for a few minutes. Each in their own thoughts, silently praying for Nehemiah's recovery.

"Thank you," Gabriella whispered. "For everything." She reached her free hand across the bed to grasp Jaclyn's and give her a gentle, yet, reassuring squeeze. Jaclyn, then, quietly left the room allowing his siblings to visit.

Two days later, Nehemiah was able to breathe on his own. While he was unconscious, Mac and Flip stopped by to talk with the family and tell them the story of what happened. They deserved to know the truth of everything.

Gabriella was shocked to find out that Nehemiah was shot charging Ortiz in an effort for him to release her. She cried more than she ever thought she could. Love was an action verb, and Nehemiah had been showing her his love in his own unique way. There was no doubt in anyone's mind that he loved her with all his heart. There was no greater love than to lay down your life for another.

She had been by his bedside every day, only leaving for a short period when she needed to. Naomi brought her a change of clothes each day, and Rachel made sure she ate. Gabriella would be eternally grateful to her sisters-in-law.

"Gabriella?" Nehemiah said, in a raspy voice.

He startled her when he spoke. She had felt his hand twitching here and there but didn't know he was awake.

"Baby, I'm here," she said.

"I know. Can I get some water?" Nehemiah asked, still not opening his eyes.

"Of course." She scrambled around the room to get the water pitcher and a cup. She only allowed him to take a few sips, but that was all he needed.

He grabbed her hand and pulled her closer. "I love you."

"I know," she smiled. Her voice was shaky. She was apprehensive about asking him a nagging question that kept popping up in her mind.

"Gabriella, say it," he coughed. "Whatever it is that is stressing you, just say it," Nehemiah told her.

He knew her so well. He hadn't opened his eyes, but somehow knew she was nervous about something.

"Why did you do it? Why did you charge Ortiz, knowing he would shoot you? Knowing you may not survive. The bullet could have hit you in the head." She was rambling and fidgeting with her hands.

He finally opened his eyes and stared at her, "Gabriella, I had to save you. Our girls need their mother."

"They need their father, too," she started crying, again.

"You are the better parent. You have been with them every day, and I only come and go as I can, but that stops now. I want to be a full-time father and a full-time husband." His breathing became labored as he talked.

"You need your rest, please. Don't talk anymore. We want to take you home soon."

His eyes closed briefly and opened again; then, he gazed at Gabriella. "Home is where I am with you." He, then, drifted off to sleep, again.

Nehemiah drifted in and out of sleep for a few days. On the day the doctors released him to travel, he was fully awake and alert. He had been in the San Juan Hospital for 17 days. His siblings were there for the first few days, and then, Moses had to return to his wife and newborn. Elijah left a day later for the same reason. His father convinced his sisters to go home, leaving only his parents, and his oldest brother, Aaron, to stay with the girls and Gabriella.

Chapter 17

Rachel had returned to Atlanta with Elijah after spending a week in Puerto Rico with Nehemiah and her family. She was packing up her things from her brother's house, preparing to return to Miami. She had several meetings rescheduled due to her travels and could, now, no longer avoid them. She still had a company to run. With Nehemiah recovering in Puerto Rico and preparing to come home soon, she could try to return to her busy life of running a music company.

While in San Juan, she had received a few text messages from Scott. Some of the messages were checking on her, and some were checking on Nehemiah. She appreciated that he was concerned, not only for her, but her family, as well. Family meant everything to her.

She had ordered a car service to take her to the airport, and it was due to arrive at any minute. Rachel went through the house in search of her brother and sister-in-law to tell them goodbye. She was heading for the backyard when she heard voices in the kitchen.

"Have you told your sister yet?" Karyn asked Scott.

"Yeah, she knows. I thought I could be happy here."

"Does your leaving have anything to do with Rachel?" Karyn inquired further.

"Why would you ask me that?" he replied, with a smile.

"Oh, something tells me there is more than a job taking you back to Miami."

Rachel fully walked into the kitchen, making them aware of her presence. "You're going back to Miami? Why?"

This was the first time she had heard of him returning to Miami. By the sounds of what she heard, he had another job. She was confused, and her face showed it.

"Karyn, do you mind if I talk to Rachel alone?"

"No. Go right ahead." Karyn grabbed a baby monitor from the kitchen island where they were sitting and walked outside into the backyard.

"Rachel, have a seat." Scott motioned toward the chair Karyn had just vacated. "I have been thinking about this since I started at Diaz. I like the people and the work, but a desk job is not really my cup of tea. I'm more suited for movement and action. While I cannot be someone's personal bodyguard, I can do surveillance type of work. I talked to Jake, and he has a position for me in the Miami office."

She didn't want to appear too excited that he would be working for her brother's company and he would back in Miami with her. "That sounds great. But where does that leave Ric?" she asked.

"I'm glad you asked that. I'll still be contracted to work for Diaz, but I'll be able to do most of my work remotely." He reached for her hands before continuing. "Besides, Ric is thinking of expanding to South Florida. Shhh, keep that quiet."

She didn't know what to say next. What she really wanted to know was, what did this change mean for them? They had been enjoying getting to know each other. Did he want to continue with their dating? She hadn't realized she was biting her lip until Scott released her hand and tipped her chin upward.

"Hey, stop that. I like your lips just the way they are."

That made Rachel blush and lower her head, again. She was about to ask him about their future when Elijah burst into the room with a screaming EJ.

"Where is Karyn?" he asked, exasperatedly.

"Out back. What's wrong?" Rachel answered.

"I don't know. EJ is not breathing right. He gasps, then cries."

Rachel jumped up from the chair and ran out back to get Karyn. Scott took action and instructed Elijah to bring the car around. Within seconds, Karyn was running through the house looking for Elijah and Eric. Rachel noticed that the front door was open, and tried to direct Karyn outside, assuming that's where they had gone. Karyn, then, started in the direction of the nursey to get Erica.

"Karyn! I'll take care of Erica and Jaleel," Rachel yelled. "You just go."

They quickly hugged, and Karyn raced for the front door.

Rachel went into the nursey to find a whimpering baby Erica. She must have known something was going on with her twin brother. Rachel picked her up from the crib and held her close, whispering that everything would be alright. They both needed to believe that.

The Boldens were a praying family, and they believed prayer worked, so Rachel walked around the house holding Erica and praying for healing and strength. They were going to need it.

Scott pulled up to the emergency room doors in record time. Karyn jumped out of the vehicle before it stopped moving and ran into the hospital screaming for help. Scott helped Elijah out of the truck while he was holding EJ.

A doctor and a nurse followed Karyn from the hospital and met Elijah at the door. They immediately took EJ from his arms and ran back into the building with Elijah and Karyn following right on their heels.

Everything happened so fast. Scott was nearly at a loss for what to do next. He stood next to the truck for a few seconds, attempting to gather his wits. There was an eerie calm outside with a gentle breeze. He noticed it was quiet and everything seemed still amid chaos. Scott parked the car in the visitor parking lot, and then, called Rachel to let her know they made it safely.

"Hey, we made it; and the doctors took them back immediately."

"Thank you, Jesus. How is EJ?" she asked with a sigh of relief.

"He was still gasping a little between cries, and boy can that baby cry," Scott softly laughed at how the crying didn't seem to bother him. It was more like a strange comfort. As long as he was crying, then he was alive.

"Ok, good. I called Moses. He and Neiko are on their way."

"How are you doing? Are you okay with Erica and Jaleel?"

"Jaleel is still taking a nap. When he wakes, I'm going to see if he wants to go swimming. As for Erica, well, me and this cutie are just bouncing around the house."

Scott smiled at the thought of Rachel and a baby. He could see her walking around their house singing to their baby. That was an image he was growing very fond of. He realized it was the only thoughts he had been having as of lately.

"Let me know if you need anything. As soon as Moses gets here, I'll head back to you," Scott told her.

"Don't worry about us. We are good."

Within minutes of ending his call with Rachel, Moses and Neiko entered the emergency room lobby. Neiko was already back to her pre-pregnancy size and looked amazing for just giving birth four weeks ago.

Moses turned to his wife and said, "You go back there with them. I'll stay out here with Scott for a few minutes." He kissed her, and she went through the doors to find Karyn and Elijah.

Moses took the seat next to Scott and patted him on the back. "I'm glad you were there when they needed you. I don't know what I would do if something happened to one of my kids. If I know my brother, he probably went crazy."

"It was no problem. Elijah was cool, but I thought Karyn was going to try and drive from the passenger seat." Scott tried to lighten the mood. "Where are your kids?"

"Nico was at a playdate with one of Neiko's friends. She offered to keep him a little while longer for us. And, Moses Jr. is at the house with Mrs. Kensington, our nanny."

They sat in amicable silence for a few minutes. The waiting room was quiet; only one other family was there. It wasn't chaotic like he had seen in movies. There was a television in the corner and books on the tables. There was even a play area for children. It reminded him of a doctor's office, and not an emergency room.

Scott was waiting for Moses to start with the questions. The news had to have traveled through the siblings. If Elijah and Nehemiah knew about him and Rachel dating, then he was pretty sure the other brothers and sisters knew, as well. They were a close family like that.

"I've been watching you with my sister. What's going on with you two?" Moses asked.

Scott had the same talk with Elijah and Nehemiah; he knew it was just a matter of time before he had to have the same talk with Moses and Aaron.

"I care about her, a lot," Scott replied.

"Enough to deal with her assertiveness and her ambitiousness? She can be all work and no play sometimes."

Scott made sure to look Moses in the eye when he answered, "I've noticed, but I think I can handle the boss lady."

Moses patted him on the back and smiled. Scott assumed that was his way of accepting their relationship.

A few minutes later Elijah came into the waiting room and plopped down onto one of the chairs next to his brother.

"I think I need a drink," he said.

"That bad?" Scott asked. He knew Elijah didn't drink anything harder than coffee.

"Man, I thought I was going to lose it. I was trying to keep it together. Karyn was, she was…" He couldn't finish his statement, Elijah dropped his head into his hands. "They are going to keep him overnight for observation. They aren't sure what happened. He wasn't choking on anything."

"Let's just thank God for the blessing that you got here in time and he is alive," Moses said.

"When I think of what could have happened had I not went into the nursery when I did…" Elijah started crying. Moses put his arm around his brother and pulled him closer.

Scott wasn't used to seeing this type of care and tenderness between men. He was taught that men who cried were weak. He was supposed to be strong and brave, not ever showing fear. When his father died, his uncles took him into a room and told him that he was the man of the family and to leave the crying to the women. Now, he was starting to learn a lot about love and family from being around the Boldens.

He hadn't cried when his father died, he hadn't cried when his grandparents passed, he hadn't even cried when he thought he might lose his only sister to cancer, but seeing these men openly share their emotions and hurt didn't make them any less of a man. Being vulnerable was an act of courage and not weakness. Scott recognized that the stereotype was just that, an overgeneralized belief and assumption made about a group of people. He would no longer subscribe to that belief. He had been learning so much from the Boldens.

"I assume you are staying overnight. I'll go back to the house and check on Rachel and grab you and Karyn a change of clothes." Scott offered. He, then, stood to leave, wanting to give the brothers time alone.

"Thank you, Scott." Elijah stood with him and embraced him in a hug. "I appreciate everything. I hope to be seeing you around a lot more often," he smiled.

Scott returned his smile and said, "You can count on it."

He returned to Elijah's house and found Rachel asleep on the sofa in the family room. Erica was in her bassinet and Jaleel was quietly watching an animated movie. Jaleel heard him enter and turned, placing a finger over his lips. He tried to whisper but failed. "Shhh, auntie is asleep."

"No, I'm not. I'm awake." Rachel took her time easing her way into a sitting position. "How is EJ?"

Scott noticed how beautiful she was even after waking up. Her hair was messy but that only added to her beauty. She had a glow he had never really seen before. It made her appear delicate and angelic. She had changed into an oversized t-shirt and a pair of jeans.

"Scott, did you hear me? How is EJ?"

"Oh, they are keeping him overnight for observation, but they don't think it is anything serious. Just being cautious. I came back to grab a few things for Elijah and Karyn. Do you mind getting her things? I feel awkward going through her clothes."

"Sure, I'll put some things in a bag for her." She stretched when she stood, and then, yawned. "I guess I was a little tired. I'll get their things. Can you watch Erica and Jaleel?"

"Of course." Scott waited for Rachel to leave the room before sitting where she had just been asleep. He peeked into the bassinet to see a smiling Erica. She was wide awake and staring right into his eyes. She made a couple of funny faces, and then, suddenly, an odor unlike any other seeped into the air.

"Oh my God! Rachel!" Scott yelled.

"What? What is it?" she ran back into the room.

"Erica pooped," Jaleel nonchalantly said, never taking his face away from the television.

"A beautiful little girl should never smell like that. What do you feed her?"

Rachel laughed at Scott and his antics. She handed him the diaper bag that was at the other end of the sofa.

Holding the bag in front of him, he asked, "What do I do with this?"

"Change her diaper. What do you think?" She reached into the bag and handed him the items he would need. "Diaper, baby wipes, diaper cream, and new pajamas if she needs them. You can handle it, military guy." She laughed louder as she returned into the bedroom.

"Jaleel, you know how to do this?"

"Uncle Scott, I'm seven," he replied.

"Right. Okay, little poopy girl, I guess it's you and me."

After a few attempts and some unsolicited advice from Jaleel, Scott was able to get Erica cleaned, and her diaper changed. Now, he cradled her in his hand like a football, and the two of them just stared at one another.

Rachel watched Scott make several attempts at changing the baby's diaper. At one point, she thought she would have to intervene when the new diaper was causing him trouble. She figured he would get it eventually, and he did.

She couldn't tear her eyes away from the image of Scott holding a baby…their baby. She understood she was jumping the gun about their future. They barely had a dating relationship, and she already had them married with kids.

"You know, you are going to be a heartbreaker when you get older. You are gorgeous just like your auntie. Both of you have these big expressive eyes that seem to see right through my soul." Erica started smiling. Scott continued, "And, your smile and laugh are so infectious. I love to hear her laugh. Do you think you can help me out here? I like your auntie a lot, but I don't know what to do. I take her to lunch and dinner, but I don't think it's enough.

She might not say it, but I know she wants me to like her career and be all excited about it, but I don't. I don't like the idea of her being around all those men. They're drooling and ogling her. See Erica, I'm getting mad just thinking about it. What am I supposed to do? I love your auntie."

"Get over it," Jaleel said, turning away from his movie.

"What did you say?"

"I said get over it. If you really do love Aunt Rachel, then you will get over whatever fears or doubts you have about her. Trust God with your whole heart and don't try to understand anything. Let God lead you."

"And, how do you know this?"

"Uncle Elijah is in school to be a minister. He teaches me...duh." And, with that, Jaleel returned to his movie.

"Out of the mouth of babes." Scott closed his eyes for a second, and then, gazed at Erica, again.

Rachel listened to the interaction he was having with Jaleel and Erica. She was excited to hear his feelings for her. They had been dancing around that subject for a while, and now he finally said it, but to an infant and a child. She wanted him to say it to her.

She entered the family room, trying to appear indifferent like she hadn't heard anything. "Here is everything they should need for an overnight stay." She exchanged the duffle bag for the baby.

"What did you pack? They're only staying for one night." Scott remarked at how heavy the bag felt.

"Ha ha. It's just the necessities. Erica, did Uncle Scott take care of you? Is your diaper on the right way?" she teased.

"Yes, it is. Thanks for helping," he sarcastically remarked.

Rachel looked at Scott, and for the first time, she saw the love that he had for her. It was clearly visible in his eyes and took her breath away. Why hadn't she noticed it before? It didn't matter, she saw it now.

"After I take this to the hospital, I'll be right back, and I want to talk to you. Will that be okay?"

He was staring at her with those intense eyes and the smile that would make her soften. If she weren't holding Erica in her arms, she might have fainted on the spot. He had that kind of effect on her.

"Yes," she breathlessly answered.

Chapter 18

Nehemiah had been in his parent's home resting for four days. He was getting frustrated with the way everyone was treating him like an invalid. Upon his release, he had slight paralysis of his left side. Each day, with physical therapy, he regained a little more strength. Now, he was able to sit up on his own, but not yet ready to stand unassisted. He was given a walker that he refused to use, and a cane he hadn't tried yet.

His mother checked on him every hour between 8 A.M. and 10 P.M. His father tried to come up with different reasons to come into his room to check on him. Once, he had needed to check the ventilation; another time, he came in to test the fire detector. Nehemiah caught on quickly, after his father used the same excuse twice.

Ruth and her children returned to their Virginia home so both, she and Naomi, came by every day. Gabriella tried to restrict the girl's access to him, saying they were causing him undue stress. To the contrary, his daughters were giving him life. He wanted to play with them and to take them to the park, instead of lying in bed watching movies and reading stories.

The physical therapist spent 3 hours a day putting his body through a rigorous workout. All he wanted was to walk again and do the basic things he had taken for granted. Depression was beginning to set in. He was feeling so down about what he couldn't do, that he forgot to be thankful for what he could do.

"Can I come in?" Jaclyn asked after knocking on the door.

"Hasn't stopped you before," he said under his breath.

"I'll ignore that. I saw your therapist just left. Are you ready for your shower?"

"Mom! I'm not letting you help me in the shower."

"Boy, I've seen everything you have."

"Not since I've been grown." He said that with a laugh.

Jaclyn sat on the side of his bed and smiled at her son. Her middle child. Boy number three. "I feel like you need some encouragement."

"Nah, Mom, I'm okay."

"Nah, Son," she imitated him. "I want you to hear this. I know we are frustrating you by constantly checking on you. That's love, Nehemiah. We do it because we love you."

Nehemiah knew she was right. She always was. All the years he tried to prove her wrong about one thing or another, she was always right. Yet, she never boasted. That was another lesson she taught her children, never brag or boast.

"Mom, I'm sorry."

"About what baby?"

"You've always stood by me, even when I was difficult to deal with. And, then, I bring this whole mess to your front door. Even now, I feel like you should be yelling at me, but you are your everyday self. Cool, calm and collected."

"Oh, Honey, I have yelled, I've screamed, but mostly, I've prayed for you. You are your own man, and I knew if I tried to stop you or persuade you in any way, you would rebel. You had to find your own way."

"Mom, I have something else to tell you. Something that happened when I was a teenager."

"You mean that little scuffle you had with the couple that used to live behind us?"

Completely astounded, his mouth hung open for a second. "How did you know about that?"

Shaking her head and laughing, Jaclyn replied, "All of you kids tried to hide things from me. Thought you had gotten away with things just because I didn't say anything. I knew all about you trying to save that woman. And, I know you confided in Elijah. What you didn't know was the mailman came by the house later that day and told me everything. He convinced the woman to get away from her husband and seek help. Your dad and a few other guys from the neighborhood helped her pack up everything and move that night."

Jaclyn grabbed her son's hands and squeezed really tight. "You were always meant to save lives. It's ingrained in the fabric of the man you are."

"But I failed, Mom. I failed." For the first time, he cried about losing Chrystal.

"What do you mean you failed? Gabriella is safe, you are alive, your team is alive."

"No, Mom. I failed Chrystal." She stared at him, waiting for him to continue. "She was a team member. We were on a mission, and we found out she was a double agent; or so we thought. We never really found out her real involvement. Anyway, she was murdered right in front of me. I couldn't save her." Nehemiah leaned into his mother and cried like he did as a child. She wrapped her arms around him and rocked him back and forth. The soothing rocking worked on her children when they were younger, and it still worked today. There was nothing like a mother's warm embrace.

She squeezed him in a big, hearty hug. "That wasn't your fault, and you know you couldn't have stopped what happened to her. This is what has caused you to look tormented at times and lose sleep at night?"

He looked at her, again, amazed at how much she knew or could see without being told anything.

She continued, "I think when you really look at the situation, that awful event you had to endure was for a reason. It made you stronger, it made you understand love better, it brought you to where you needed to be in your life. It prepared you for future missions."

They sat, embraced, for several more minutes without saying anything. Nehemiah reflected on everything that has happened to him since Chrystal's death. And, again, his mother was spot on. He did learn from that event. He was better in his job, and his protective instincts heightened. From that, he was able to discern that Gabriella needed his help, and he was able to recognize love again when it smacked him in the face.

Jaclyn wiped the tears from his eyes. "Remember, love lifted you."

Leave it to his mom to give him a whopping dose of good ole faith. She always knew what to say at the right time. And to think, all these years he and Elijah thought they shared a secret. That thought made him laugh, and he was still laughing when Gabriella entered the room after his mother left.

"Are you okay?" she asked.

"Yeah, Baby, I'm fine. My mom is a character, always has been." He patted the side of the bed where his mom had previously sat. "Come here, I want to talk to you."

When she sat down, he pulled her to his chest and held her tightly, so she couldn't move away.

"I am too much weight to have on top of you."

"Baby, you are as light as a feather. I want to tell you something."

"I know you love me. I love you, too." He had been saying that to her a lot since he regained consciousness in the hospital.

"Nope, that's not what I was going to say. I was going to say that as soon as I am walking on my own with no assistance, I want you to have the wedding of your dreams." She was about to speak, but he stopped her. "And, I want another baby as soon as possible. I'm going to need to keep up with my siblings."

"Are you sure?"

"Am I sure I want to make all of your dreams come true? Yes. Am I sure I want another baby?" he paused. "I want as many kids as you want to give me."

Gabriella started crying, and then, she laughed. He was going to make her dreams come true. She had mentioned, once, that she had never had a wedding; and, now, he wanted to give her that.

Nehemiah's family loved him; how could he be depressed with all of their love surrounding him and his family? His mother said to remember love lifted him, and that was very true. Love lifted him.

*****

When Scott returned to the hospital, both Elijah and Moses pulled him into a private room and told him, if he was serious about Rachel, he had their blessing. Then, they prayed with him...not *for* him, but *with* him. His mother had prayed for him, his sister had prayed for him, but there was a difference when someone prayed with you.

Immediately after praying, Scott instantly knew what he wanted and what he wanted to do. He even knew how he wanted to do it. He would date her properly in Miami and make sure she knew they were exclusive. He would give her no more than a year, and then, he would propose to her. He wanted her to see him and really fall in love with him.

Scott returned to the house, after leaving the hospital a second time, to find Rachel asleep on the sofa. This time, Jaleel had gone to bed, and Erica was sound asleep in her bassinet. He stared at her while she slept. He had a chance to really think about his future and what he wanted in his life. She was definitely what he wanted.

He stared down at her and saw his future. Not wanting to scare her, he gently stroked her shoulder and softly called her name.

"Hey, you're back," she whispered. "I didn't mean to fall asleep. I never knew an infant could wear you out like this. Karyn is definitely a superwoman."

"Yes, she is," Scott agreed with her. He reached down and grabbed Rachel's hand. "Let's go into the kitchen and talk. Besides, I'm starving. And, I know you're hungry."

Together, they prepared turkey and cheese sandwiches and a fruit salad. They blessed their food before Scott started talking.

"Rachel, I learned something today. Actually, I knew it in my heart weeks ago, but it took a little time to make it to my head. I'm in love with you. I didn't want to accept it in Miami. That's why I left. I was running from all of these feelings and emotions I have never felt before."

Rachel sat quietly, eating her sandwich, not wanting to interrupt.

"But I know that I can't run from my heart any longer. I can't run from you. I love you. I want us to exclusively date, get to know each other better, and take this relationship one day at a time. I want to marry you, and I want to have a family with you." He started shaking his head. She looked like a cat caught with the canary in its mouth. He wasn't sure what she was thinking, but he wanted her to know his true feelings and intentions.

"I don't want to rush you into anything. I just want you to know where I'm coming from. What I need to know from you is, what do you want?"

"Yes...yes. I want everything you want. Everything you just said, I want it, too. Before you left Miami, I knew I loved you. I prayed, and I talked to my mother and my sister and even Karyn. I didn't know how I could love you so fast, but I did. They all said it's possible."

He grabbed her hand, causing her to drop the sandwich she was still holding. Pulling her into his arms and warm embrace, he kissed her forehead, and then, each cheek, before softly kissing her lips. "We take this slow and really get to know one another. No rush, understood?" he said.

"I like that," she replied.

Chapter 19

One Year Later

The Bolden estate was packed with every Bolden family member they could find. This was a family reunion like none other. The families of all of Jeremiah's siblings were represented this year. Eleven of his brothers and sisters were in attendance; their oldest brother Justin had died a few years earlier. Forty-eight of their fifty-one children were in attendance, and there were too many grandchildren and great-grandchildren to count.

At midnight, the night before, Gabriella had the wedding of her dreams as promised by her husband. She wore a one-of-a-kind Victoria Bolden design. Victoria Bolden was one of their many cousins. The dress was an empire silhouette, with a waistline just below the bustline. It effectively hid the small baby-bump Gabriella was sporting.

Her bridesmaids were her loving sisters-in-law, and her daughters were the flower girls. She walked down the aisle alone, but when the minister asked, "Who gives this woman away to be wed?" all of the Bolden men in attendance stood and said, "We do."

There was no reception; a simple champagne toast was all that was needed. There would be plenty of festivities to celebrate their union and the many other announcements that were to be shared throughout the weekend.

Scott finally got around to properly proposing to Rachel. There would be another wedding by the end of the year. Monica had a healthy baby boy who they named, Dominic. Karyn was pregnant again, and her twins were barely walking. Moses had mentioned wanting another child, but Neiko put an ax in that idea quickly.

The family was spread across every inch of his yard; and Jeremiah Bolden would not want it any other way. He loved his family and never tired of having them around. They were getting ready for the 3-on-3, old school vs. new school basketball game. Due to the number of participants, they were competing bracket-style just like the annual spades and bid-whist tournament they held during Thanksgiving.

Before the start of the basketball game, Jeremiah grabbed the microphone from the DJ to make an announcement.

"Family! Please gather around. I have some very important news to share with everyone." He waited for most of the family to come closer. "One year ago, this week, I almost lost my son, Nehemiah. He was shot trying to protect his family. Like every one of us here, family is everything, and there is nothing we wouldn't do for family. We may not always get along, and we rarely agree on anything…"

"Except family reunions here, Uncle Jeremiah!" someone from the back yelled out, causing a chuckle among the family.

"You got that right, but even though we argue, fuss, and fight we still love each other. A scripture came to me this morning. Psalm 127:3-5. Now, I'm paraphrasing for the young folks, but it says that our children are God's legacy, and they are the best gifts

He has given to us. We are blessed to be parents to all of you. Our enemies don't stand a chance against us, family!"

A chorus of amens were heard throughout the backyard.

"Before we start with the competitive trash-talking, let's recite our family scripture. All the young people who don't know it by memory, I'll give you a minute to pull out your phones. It's first Corinthians 13:4-8 & 13. I will say 'love,' and you finish the statement.

Love – *is patient*

Love – *is kind*

Love – *does not envy*

Love – *does not boast*

Love – *is not proud*

Love – *does not dishonor others*

Love – *is not self-seeking*

Love – *is not eagerly angered*

Love – *it does not keep record of wrongs*

Love – *does not delight in evil*

Love – *rejoices with truth*

Love – *always protects, always trusts, always hopes, always perseveres*

Love – *never fails*

Verse 13, all together – *And now these three remain: faith, hope, and love, but the greatest of these is love.*

Amen."

ABOUT THE AUTHOR

Lisa Washington is a Contemporary Christian Fiction author and a serial entrepreneur. She is the co-founder of the Washington Way LLC, which is the umbrella company for Washington Way Publishing, Washington Way Travel, Washington Way Financial and Ms. Lisa Weddings.

Her first novel *When You Least Expect It* received an African American Literary Show Award for Best Christian Fiction. She has also published *More Than You Know*, which is the second novel of the Faith Series.

Lisa Washington was born and raised in Detroit, Michigan. After serving in the United States Navy, she then went on to obtain a Bachelor of Arts from Wayne State University, an MBA from Averett University and an MFA in creative writing from Butler University.

She now resides in Noblesville, Indiana with her family.

JOIN MY MAILING LIST

Did you enjoy Love Lifted Me? Write a review for Amazon & Goodreads. Let other readers know that you enjoyed it and they will to.

www.authorlisawashington.com

Also, join my mailing list to receive messages from me about new releases, sneak peeks, sales, contests and giveaways.

Click here to join